The Little Fishes

THE
LITTLE
FISHES

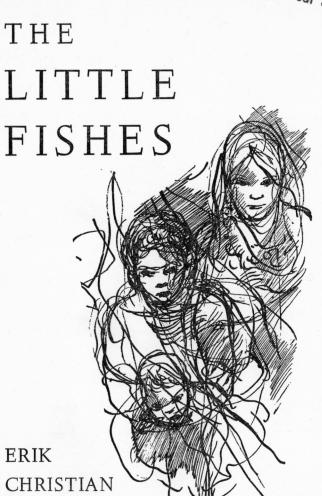

ERIK
CHRISTIAN
HAUGAARD

Illustrated by Milton Johnson

HOUGHTON MIFFLIN COMPANY BOSTON

Books by
Erik Christian Haugaard

Hakon of Rogen's Saga
A Slave's Tale
Orphans of the Wind

THIRD PRINTING   C

CONTENTS

To Liliana and Menenio Codella

Preface

"TELL ME about the war. What was it like?" the child asks his father, and the father looks away trying to remember.

Faces come to him: young faces of friends who never became fathers to be asked the question, "What was it like?"

"Oh, it was bad," the father finally replies; and then because he is a kind man, he tells about a humorous incident that happened to him during the war: for even when life is misery, a man must laugh.

This is the story of three children and their Odyssey from Naples to Cassino, in 1943. It is a grim story, an unhappy story, a lesson in history, as it was written in the minds and hearts of those to whom it was taught. I hope also that it is an answer to that query, "What was it like?" which most veterans leave unanswered.

"The Little Fishes"

"When you boil unclean water, it will form a scum on its surface." The captain looked at me and the other children with disgust. "There is the scum!" With a clean, slender finger he pointed at me, probably because I stood nearest to him.

I held out my hand and mumbled, "Signor Capitano, we are starving."

The officer turned toward his companion, a German, who smiled not unkindly at me. "Who knows . . ." he started to say in broken Italian. "Who knows what water is unclean?"

"The Italy that produced Caesar is buried in the dirt of poverty and beggars. Naples!" The captain spat the word out as if he were saying a curse.

The German did not reply. He was staring at us

children. There were at least ten of us. Carefully he took out of his small leather purse one coin and threw it among us. It fell so far away from me that I knew I would not have any chance to grab it, so I did not join the heap of sprawling arms and legs. I stood still watching the officers.

One of the smaller boys cried out as one of the older ones kicked him. At that sound a slight smile passed over the foreigner's face. "Don't you think there were any beggars when the Caesars reigned?" he asked the captain, taking out another coin to throw among us.

This time the coin fell quite near me and my instinct — acquired from having passed so many days without food — made me wish to throw myself upon it; but I didn't. A voice within me asked, why, and I could not answer.

"Naturally, there were beggars then; but not like this!"

The German officer yawned as if the captain bored him; and at that moment, I realized that his feeling towards the captain was the same as the captain's feeling towards us.

The second coin, a girl managed to snatch. Now she stood eagerly watching the German, waiting for him to throw another. The little boy who had cried out walked up to the German. The boy's hand was filled with dirt from the street. He showed it to the German. "Capitano, I will eat this, if you will pay."

The German nodded and smiled, while he held up

a small coin between two of his fingers. The child stuck the filth into his mouth and tried to swallow it; but it was too dry. He coughed and spat it out. The German laughed and the other children laughed with him. The boy started to cry again and the officer gave him the coin.

I had not laughed and sometimes silence is louder than laughter, for now the German was looking at me. He selected a large coin and threw it. It rolled to within an inch of my right foot. All I had to do was place my foot upon it and it would be mine. I didn't; while my brain shouted "With that you can buy a whole bread!" my foot kicked it away.

The German laughed and even the Italian captain smiled. "Now you shan't get any," the foreigner said thoughtfully. I nodded to show that I understood. "In the unclean waters live the little fishes. Some are eaten; most, I believe. But some will escape." And with a mock salute the German turned from us. The Italian captain followed him, and they both walked down the street.

Most of the children ran after them. The boy who had offered to eat dirt and the girl who had caught the second coin remained behind. The boy opened his hand to look at his coin and the girl snatched it from him; even before he could start to cry, she was gone.

Tears ran from his eyes down his dirty cheeks, like little rivers through a dusty landscape. I thought, 'Some people's faces are made to smile and

laugh. Some are made for anger. And his little face
was made for tears.'

"Little fishes," I repeated the words of the German aloud.

The boy kept on crying. Now he was sitting on
the curb. He had rubbed his face with his hands,
and the tears and dirt had mixed. I walked over to
him. I had seen him before but I did not know his
name. I wanted to tell him that he could not have
bought much with that coin, but I knew that it was
not for the money alone he was crying.

Suddenly the boy looked up at me and spoke
through his sobs, "It was my sister." The telling of
this fact brought on new tears.

Roughly, with no kindness in my voice, I said,
"Stop it."

The little boy put his hands up in front of his face,
but he did stop crying.

"Come with me," I ordered. Without looking
back to see whether he was following me, I started
walking towards the Church of St. ———.

The beggar evaluates all other human beings ac-
cording to their generosity, as you judge a spring
from the amount of water it gives. To the starving,
only food has value; hunger supplants all other feel-
ings . . . What I have just told you is not com-
pletely true. You should beware, for often in this
story, my words will be spoken out of bitterness,

out of hate. The scream of the poor is not always just; but if you do not listen to it, then you will never understand justice.

In the Church of St. ——— there were three priests: Don Carlo, who was young and a favorite among the young girls, they flocked to his confession box; Don Armando was, as most people are, interested in feathering his own nest, making it warm and comfortable for himself; then there was an elderly priest, *il vecchio* . . . "the old one," as most people called him. His cassock was usually dirty and some people said that his mind was gone. The poor came to him to confess and he listened. Sometimes he cried; and a priest who cries most people don't respect, for tears are a sign of weakness.

The church was cool. I grabbed the boy by the shoulder and walked over to the confession box of Father Pietro, "the old one." He was confessing an old woman. She wore no shoes and from the soles of her feet, I could read that she came from the country. 'If only she gives him something,' I thought, 'not a chicken or something valuable, but a bread. A bread she baked last night to take with her to give the priest.'

The old woman mumbled on, sighed several times, and put her weight first on one knee and then on the other. I kept thinking of the bread, imagining its smell. The little boy stood next to me; his face still bore the mark of his tears. 'Good!' I thought. His little chest was covered by a torn shirt. I opened the shirt, so that the shadows made by his ribs could be seen.

At last the woman was finished. The priest spoke, but I could not catch his words; then came the benediction and the old woman crossed herself. Very slowly she got up; her knees were stiff. She looked around the church. It was dark, for who can buy candles in a city where more than half the people are starving? She made her way to the picture of the Blessed Mother and kneeled down again to pray. I hoped she wouldn't pray long, because I did not want to go to Father Pietro until she had left. As if the woman knew of my wish, she rose and disappeared through the portals of the church.

Quickly I pulled the little boy up to the confessional box. Standing beside him, I spoke through the curtain that hid the priest from our view. "Father Pietro . . . Father Pietro," I called in a loud whisper.

The old man drew the curtain and peered out. He was nearly blind and wore thick glasses.

"It is I . . . Guido . . . I have brought someone." Gently, I pushed the child toward the priest.

He leaned down to look at the boy. "*Madonna mia . . .*" he whispered, while he made the sign of the cross above the child's head.

"He is hungry."

The priest nodded. The little one had already spied the bread the woman had brought. It was only partly wrapped in paper and lay on the seat next to the priest. Slowly the priest picked the bread up and from the fold of his cassock took out a small penknife, which had been sharpened so often that there was almost no blade left. He cut the small bread in half, and gave the boy a half loaf.

The moment the boy had the bread in his hands, he glanced up at me; and his eyes had the expression of a dog who fears for the bone in his mouth.

He darted past the altar, to the darkest corner of the church, his teeth already in his bread.

I had meant to share with the boy, and I was angry. Then I heard the old priest mumble, "He forgot to cross himself." At that moment I remembered that Father Pietro came from a rich family. I had been told that he was from the north and he had given all he owned to the Church; but being a fool, he had never risen above being an ordinary priest.

"I am hungry, too, Father."

The priest looked down at me. In his one hand he still held the half loaf; in the other, his penknife. "You are a good boy, Guido. You brought him to me because he was hungry." The old man smiled at me and I smiled back; but I was thinking of the bread in his hand.

Suddenly the priest frowned. "You didn't bring him here, to beg bread from me, so you could eat it, did you?"

I looked away. "Someone had given him a coin. His sister stole it from him, and I felt sorry." As I spoke, I thought, 'It is not a lie.' I was afraid of lying to Father Pietro, although to Don Carlo I would have lied without thinking about it.

The priest took the knife and started cutting the remainder of the bread in two. My gaze followed the knife; in the middle of the piece it stopped. I glanced up at the old priest, he was looking at me intently. "I had some bread this morning and a cup of milk." The old man spoke slowly as though he were not talking to me. He drew the knife out and gave me the half loaf.

"Thank you, Father," I said hurriedly and bent my head, while my hands fondled the crust of the bread, as if I were a blind man.

"Run along," the old man said in a tired voice; and then he blessed me.

I walked slowly without taking a bite of the bread. When I reached the entrance, I dipped my hand into the Holy Water and kneeled down. I could see the altar and the old priest who was standing next to his confession box.

Once outside I bit into the bread. It was good, made from flour into which no chaff had been mixed. The sun was bright; I had no thought for anything but my bread. Suddenly I heard a voice saying, "What have you got there, boy?"

I jumped aside. Father Carlo's hand missed me.

"It is a piece of bread. Father Pietro gave it to me," I said angrily, hiding the bread behind my back and keeping myself out of the priest's reach.

"You have stolen it," he said.

I shook my head and backed down the stairs. The priest laughed. It was a sour laugh that made his handsome face appear ugly. "He would give the whole church away, the old fool. He would strip the Blessed Madonna for such little brats as you."

I knew what Don Carlo was referring to, for everyone had heard of Father Pietro's idea. He wanted to sell the golden crown of the Madonna that stood near the altar and buy bread. When I reached the bottom step, I turned ready to run. I wanted to stick my tongue out at Don Carlo, now that I was a safe distance away from him; but I was afraid that he might tell Father Pietro. I brought the loaf up to my mouth, so that he could see me taking a big bite from it. With a shrug of his shoulders, as if to say, 'I have many such loaves,' the priest turned and entered the church.

A little crust of the bread I kept in my pocket for later, when I would be going to sleep. It is hard to sleep when you are very hungry; but if you eat even a tiny piece of bread slowly, you can fool your stomach.

The grownups have their cafés; places where they go to talk, even when they don't have the money to buy a drink or a cup of coffee. The children, "the little fishes," also have their places where they meet. I was wandering towards "our" piazza. It was a small square of no particular importance, which is probably why we gathered there.

Standing a few yards away from a group of children, I recognized the girl, the sister of the little boy. She was thin and her dress was only a rag. I guessed her to be about ten years old, or a little younger. I was almost half a head taller than she was. I walked towards her, but I was keeping my glance directed towards the group of children near her.

They were discussing a robbery that had taken place in the district, a store had been broken into. I thought I knew which gang of older boys had done it; and this knowledge made me smile proudly.

"Why did you steal the coin from your brother?" It was a silly question and the girl did not answer it. "I got him half a loaf of bread," I boasted.

This time she looked up at me. Her hair was long and very dirty. "He is a stupid boy. He will die from eating dirt. Last week he ate a live caterpillar for the sake of the soldiers. He is a stupid boy. He will never grow up." She spoke with such finality that I did not disagree.

I was fingering the crust in my pocket. Suddenly to my own surprise, I broke it in two and gave the girl the smaller piece. I was so amazed at what I was doing that I watched my hand, as if it belonged to somebody else.

I had expected her to grab the bread; but she picked it up gracefully between two fingers and lifted it to her mouth. It was so small that she could have eaten it in one gulp, but she chewed for a long time before she swallowed it. "Thank you," she said. "Thank you . . . Anna . . . Anna is my name."

I didn't tell her what my name was; but I smiled, for now I was glad that I had given her the bread. "How old are you?" I asked.

She drew the number eleven with her feet in the dirt. I laughed and drew my own age beside hers.

"Twelve," she said aloud and added, "You are big for your age."

"Anna!" The girl looked up. At the corner of the square stood a small, hunched old woman; she was beckoning towards us.

"Your mother?"

The girl shook her head; and then waving her hand, by way of saying good-bye, she walked away. Within a few minutes, she had disappeared with the old woman down one of the very narrow streets that led from the square. 'I shall see her again,' I thought.

"Guido . . ." one of the boys called. "Do you know who it was?" For a moment, I thought he meant the girl; but then I realized that they were still talking about the robbery.

"Of course, I do," I answered.

Several of the children cried, "Who?"

I turned and walked away. When I reached the far corner of the piazza, I shouted to them, "It was Don Carlo!"

They all laughed and I grinned happily to myself.

Everyone Has a Home

2

THE SNAIL carries his home on his back. The lizard has his favorite crack in the wall; and masterless dogs have their dark corners, where, when night comes, they can creep, and from the smell know that this place is their own. Those who have addresses, with the names of streets and numbers that they can use to tell other people where they live, call the rest of us "homeless"; but they are wrong, for everyone of us has a home of his own.

A beggar who was called "the lame one" had

slept beneath a stairway. There he had arranged his
rags, which were so dirty that no one else would
want them. One morning he was dead; and the police called him "homeless." I heard them, for I was
there. It was I who had first realized that "the lame
one" was not sleeping but dead. He had come from
Calabria, and was always longing for his village.
When I found him dead, the first thing I thought to
myself was, 'He has returned to his village, to the
land, to his animals.' And I was not sad.

"The lame one" had thought that he had seen
God; and his brothers had sent him away from the
village because of the scandal. One Sunday during
Mass "the lame one" had called the priest a liar; and
then had asserted, when the priest had asked him
how he could think of saying such a thing, that
God had told him to say it. After that the priest had
forbidden him to enter the church. Many a time
"the lame one" had told me the story; and he had always ended it with the same sentence: "But the
church is God's, Guido. The church is God's."

I had always agreed with him, for he had done
no one any harm, and had always been so pleased
that anyone would listen to him. When the other
beggars had made fun of him, "the lame one" had
always burst into tears. What he had liked to speak
of most had been the land, which he owned with his
brothers, and their animals, especially their cow.
"Guido, she was white like the Blessed Mother, and
big. Ah, no bigger cow was there in the whole vil-

lage!" Then "the lame one" would become silent, and I had often thought that if I could have seen into his eyes at those moments there would have been a picture of the biggest cow in the village, "white like the Blessed Mother."

"The lame one's" home had been under the stairs of a very old house. It was cold and damp. None of the beggars wanted it; and after he died, two dogs took it over: rags and all.

I do not know why I have told you the story of "the lame one." He was of no importance to anyone but himself. In one of the churches in my district is a picture of St. Joseph. The picture is made of small colored stones. One stone is missing. It is not a stone in the face of St. Joseph or even in his dress; it is in the background, near the sandal of his right foot. Yet when you look at the picture, your eyes stop at the place where the stone is missing and stay there, as if it were the most important part of the picture. Maybe if I had not told you the story of "the lame one," there would be an empty spot in my story, and you would have thought, 'There is something he should have told us, and didn't.'

Guido's house . . . my house . . . was in a cave at the foot of the mountain that rises steeply in the middle of the city. On top of that mountain, there live many rich people and the district is called Vomero. It was a small cave, in which a carpenter had his workshop and an old man, called "sack of bones," had a stable for his horse. I have said it was "my house"; but the carpenter called it his, and "sack of bones," who paid the carpenter for letting him and his horse stay there, thought it was his, as well. The truth was that none of us owned it. Every month the carpenter went off to an office in Via Roma and the notary took his money without ever telling him for whom he was collecting the rent. I, too, paid for living there by helping "sack of bones" and the carpenter. Sometimes I brushed down the horse; sometimes I ran an errand.

Each of us had his own part of the cave. The carpenter had the largest, for he was the *padrone*; "sack of bones," the little stable in the rear; and I, a corner near where the horse stood. That corner was Guido's home.

The rich man brags about how many floors his *palazzo* . . . his mansion has, about the size of the garden that surrounds it, and the rare flowers that grow there; he does not think when he passes the hovels of the poor, that also they vary in value. Advantages are as carefully measured and gloated over among the poor, as terraces and servants are among the wealthy.

Shortly after I first met Anna, I acquired a treasure that made my home seem to me much more worthwhile. I am afraid you will laugh, when I name my treasure; therefore, I shall do it quickly, as one does when one is forced to tell the truth; it is a woolen mattress. Sunny Naples can be cold, when the winter wind comes from the mountains. The palm trees down at the aquarium, battling against the wet coldness, seem to say, 'We don't belong here. We don't belong here.'

I found my mattress in a house that had been destroyed during one of the first bombardments of Naples. How long it had lain there, I don't know. The cover was torn and tufts of wool were sticking out; yet during the war any woolen mattress had value, however torn the cover. I could easily have found a buyer for it, but from the first moment I saw it, I wanted it for myself, for Guido's home.

I could not carry the mattress alone all the way to the cave; it was too heavy. I would have to get someone to help me. Someone who would not take the mattress for himself, once I had shown him where it was; so I preferred someone smaller than I was. The other consideration was that it had to be taken at night because of the police. There were policemen who looked the other way, when they saw us, even if we were carrying something obviously not our own; but there were others who hated the beggar children.

As soon as I climbed out of the bombed building, I made my way to "our" piazza. It was late afternoon; it would soon be dark. As always at this hour, there were many children. I sat down on the curb and watched them. I mentioned the name of each one that I knew, and then asked myself whether he was the best one to bring along that night. Renato had no shoes, would he not try to steal the mattress

from me? Luigi . . . perhaps, but wasn't he too
small? Each time I rejected a name, I thought of the
mattress lying there, where someone else might
take it.

From one of the side streets, Anna entered the
square. She was not tall; yet I knew that she must
be strong, and that together we could carry the mattress. I had one *lira*, would she be satisfied with
that?

"Anna . . ." I called softly.

"Yes?" she asked.

I walked away and Anna followed me. She was a
clever girl and kept a few paces behind, for she
knew that when one had something of importance
to discuss, it was well that nobody else knew about
it.

I turned down a narrow street and finally Anna
hurried to catch up with me. "I have found something. Something too heavy for me to carry, would
you help me? It's a mattress."

She twirled a strand of her hair around her finger.
"I am afraid of the police," she said so matter-of-
factly that I was convinced that she was not — at
least, no more afraid than any of us were.

'She probably wants two *lire*,' I thought and
made a grimace. "It has to be done tonight," I said
aloud. "After twelve, I want to carry it to my
place." I had thought of offering her half a *lira* first,
in order to be able to make the price higher, for
it is better when the other person thinks he has

made you pay more than you intended. But I was
so anxious that I burst out, "I will give you a *lira*,
if you help me."

She looked away. "A mattress is heavy," she argued.

"But it is not very far," I said quickly.

I had to wait for her, but she did meet me as
she had promised. The moon shone down on the
ruins of the house. "There it is," I said and pointed
towards the corner.

Anna glanced at the mattress, then she looked up
at the moon. "Guido, I don't like it here."

I laughed at her, though the silence and the shadows which the broken beams and the tumbled walls
cast upon the floor frightened me as well. "Come," I
said in a hushed voice, as one speaks when one
passes a churchyard at night.

I grabbed hold of one end of the mattress and she of the other. "It is heavy, Guido. Let's let it be," she whispered.

"You promised!" I shouted at her; and then, as if in defiance of the night, I repeated as loudly as before, "You promised!"

With difficulty, we got the mattress over the ruined walls. The night was cold. The streets empty and dark. It took us more than an hour to reach the cave; several times, we had to stop and rest.

Our cave had a large portal, but in one of the doors was a smaller door which we always used at night. It was large enough to drag the mattress through, but even Anna had to bend her head to enter. The horse whinnied, when she heard us; but I spoke to her and she recognized my voice.

In my corner was a little wooden box, and in it I kept the things I valued. Now I opened it and brought out the stump of a candle and lighted it. The flickering light cast great shadows, but this was my home; its dark corners were empty of fear. The smell of the horse and the warmth from it made my corner cozy.

"It's a good place." The admiration in Anna's tone made me proud. I patted the horse on its rump; it switched its tail into my face and made the girl laugh.

We put the mattress in the corner next to my box, and we both lay down on it. "It is a good place,"

Anna repeated. "I shall come here, when my aunt throws me out."

"Would she throw you out?" I asked.

"I don't know," she said.

"If she does, you can come here," I invited; though I regretted that I had had to say it, for I did not want to share my home with anyone.

Anna nodded. "Give me my *lira*."

I took the *lira* from a pocket on the inside of my jacket and gave it to her. She looked at it and then stuffed it inside her dress. I opened the little door for her. Anna shivered as she stepped outside.

"Thank you," I said; and I stood in the doorway listening to her steps as she walked down the deserted street.

My little candle was not quite burned down. I found the two sacks, which I used as covers; and threw them over me. I was about to blow out the candle, to save what was left of it; but suddenly — for no reason whatever — I wanted to let it burn. For four or five minutes, I lay with the light of the candle, expecting at any second that it would sputter and go out. Finally, it flickered and the wick fell into the last little pool of wax. 'It is because of the mattress,' I thought, 'that is why I let it burn.'

A Beggar's Day

3

"TROUBLE, GUIDO, and misery; that is life. We are but a sack of bones that God has given life to!"

I could not help smiling when the old man said that, for it was from this, his favorite expression, "we are but a 'sack of bones,'" he had gotten his nickname. It was a chilly morning in January, 1943. The old man was getting his horse ready for work. The animal was a mare, well past her prime. She was at least fifteen years old, and had come to that age when a horse grows thin, regardless how much food it gets. "Sack of bones" fed his horse as well as he could; often he would even share his bread with her.

"My little beauty." The old man caressed the mare while he put the harness on her. She stood perfectly still; her big brown eyes looked sadly at the open doors of the cave. "My beauty, it is no weather for working. But what are we to do? We must work or we don't eat." The mare turned her head towards the old man; and I almost expected it to speak, to say something like, 'Ah, my handsome one, life is trouble.' The accord between the two was such that they seemed always to be in the same mood. I had never seen the old man hit the animal. He made me think of St. Francis preaching to the birds. Yet "sack of bones" was not like St. Francis, for he did not love any other animal but his mare. He feared dogs and would throw stones after them.

The old man thought of the world as evil. "He is like a hermit in the middle of a city," Father Pietro once said of him. Between these two men there was a strange familiarity. They would hold long conversations together, when they met in the streets, yet I do not think that old "sack of bones" ever went to Mass. Maybe it was the fact that the rest of the world thought of both of them as fools that made them friends. I have sometimes thought that "sack of bones'" hatred of the world and the priest's love of it sprang from the same childlike heart.

I helped the old man harness the mare to his cart, and then watched him as he led the horse down the street towards the harbor. "Sack of bones" never stood in the cart himself; he always walked beside the great wheels holding the reins, even when the cart was empty.

My life then consisted of the day that had already dawned; tomorrow was another world, a world only those who had work dared contemplate. The carpenter had not come, for he had no wood. An old cart that he was supposed to repair stood in front of the cave. I closed the portals and walked back to my bed to lay down. I had had nothing to eat the night before, and my hunger made me more aware of the cold of the morning. I drew the sacks over me; but even though I was wearing all the clothes that I owned — I wore my old pants on top of the ones I usually wore — I felt cold.

God has so arranged it that the poor, who can ill afford guests, usually have plenty of them. All of Naples was filled with fleas then; and even the rich, who lived in Vomero, sometimes had them. It made me laugh to see a rich man; or an officer; or a woman, who had a servant following her to carry her parcels, stop to scratch themselves, when they thought that no one was looking. The rich who eat well really should have all the fleas, for their blood must be fatter than ours. I scratched my chest, but then my back itched; finally, because I could find no comfort, I got up.

"My father died in Africa. He was a soldier, Signor Capitano. I am hungry!"

The lieutenant I had been following down the street looked away, as if he had not heard me. And though I had shouted, as I ran to keep up with him, had he heard me? How many children had already told him the same story that morning?

"For Italy, Signor Capitano. Give me something for God, Country, and Family."

The officer stopped and looked down at me. "For Italy!" he said bitterly and laughed. *"Dio, Patria, e Famiglia* . . . even the beggars in Naples know that."

"It is true, Signor Capitano. My father did die in Africa." I squinted my eyes, as if I were about to cry; then opened them wide and met the lieutenant's gaze, but I said no more. As a fisherman knows when he has caught a fish, so does the beggar know when his hook has been swallowed. The officer took out his small purse. I held out my hand. He gave me fifty *centesimi.* "Thank you, Signor Capitano."

With a shrug of his shoulders and the same bitter smile as before, he said, *"Pro Patria,"* and walked away.

Also begging is an art, for the heart of each human being is like a lock, to which you must find a key. The key is not only the words you speak, but the expression on your face as well. Some people prefer to give only to happy beggars. Others want you to be miserable; your story cannot be sad enough. There are even those who are amused by

arrogance; and the good beggar can be all to everyone.

"I am an orphan. Give to the motherless. Signora, by Our Lady, have mercy on the unfortunate."
The woman I had been walking beside was dressed
all in black. Was she in mourning for her parents,
her husband, or a child? Her shoes were worn; but
then everyone's shoes were shabby, for now in the
middle of the war, even the rich did not always have
new clothes to wear.

"For the sake of Our Mother, Signora. I am hungry, Signora."

The woman glanced at me, but she averted my gaze.

"If you have no money, Signora, then pray for me. My name is Guido. I am only twelve years old. I have not eaten for two days. Pray for me!"

The woman looked across the street. Sometimes this is as good a sign as when someone looks directly at you. "Please, Signora," I said softly, almost whispering the words.

The woman rummaged in her bag; she drew out a ten *centesimi* piece, and gave it to me without looking at me. "Grazia . . . Thank you," I said very loudly, and stood still to let her pass.

At the corner, before she crossed the street, she turned for a moment to look back at me. 'It is not often that she gives anything,' I thought; and meeting her glance I grinned.

Some days are lucky and some are not: this everybody knows. Nor is it always the day that starts out well that is the best. Sometimes in the middle of the winter, you wake up to a day of sunshine that belongs to April. Today is your lucky day, you think. You cross yourself and laugh, even though you are hungry; but before noon there is a cold wind and you go to bed that night hungrier than you were when you rose in the morning. On the other hand you may wake up, thinking that no one in the world could be as miserable as you are. You drag yourself out into the streets and right away, someone calls, "Guido, help me with this." Or the first person you ask for money gives you two *lire*. Then you know that it is a special day and you get all warm inside. Out of the corner of Her eye, Our Lady is looking down at you, and you forget all the thoughts you had when you woke. This was such a day for me. By one o'clock I had enough money to buy food, and still have a whole *lira* left for the next day.

There are many places to eat in Naples; and the rich and the very poor sometimes used to eat in the same place: the rich inside at tables covered with white clothes; the poor at the rear door buying the left-overs from the cook. But by the winter of 1943, the waiters ate the left-overs, for the borders of the land of the miserable had spread. Each day there were more beggars and fewer people to beg from; more people asking for work and less work to be had. The very rich left Naples to go and live on their estates; while from the country came those who were so poor that they owned no land and had had to work for others. They smelled of mules and donkeys, and were beggars as soon as they entered Naples.

The beggars, the unfortunate, also have restaurants of their own. In some cellar or even over an open fire in the street, a woman would boil a soup of bones and vegetables, which she sold by the bowlful. I went to one of these restaurants. And truly, I was lucky that day, for my bowl had a big lump of fat in it. I ate it slowly. I could have bought more soup, but I wanted bread.

Bread was rationed, as were meats and almost everything else one needed. But the very poor had no address. They were homeless. They were not citizens of Naples. They could not register themselves, and therefore, they got no ration cards. They had to buy their ration cards or their bread on the black market; thus, those who had most need of bread were forced to pay the most for it.

I went to one of the bread stores; there was a long line outside, and I had no card. Down a little alley there was a door that led to the back of the bakery. This was usually not only closed, but locked. As I neared the door, a cart that was being drawn by a little donkey approached from behind; so narrow was the alley that I had to press myself against the door to get out of the cart's way. As I pushed my shoulders up against it, the door opened. I felt the warmth from the oven and began to sniff the smell of the bread. The cart drove by, and I stepped cautiously inside. I was in the small storeroom, where the flour and wood were kept.

There was a door from the storeroom that led into the big room where the baking was done. I could hear the men working. I tiptoed to the door and hid behind it and looked through the crack. Right near me was a rack, on which the bread that had just been taken out of the oven was set to cool. I folded my hands and prayed to Our Lady that none of the bakers would see me; for is not She, who is the Mother of God, also the Mother of Orphans? I sneaked out of my hiding place and into the bakery. I reached out my hand and placed it on a bread. I almost cried out, for it was so hot that it burned my fingers. With my arms I clutched the bread to my chest, and ran through the storeroom out into the alley.

As I closed the door behind me, I expected to hear the angry cries of "stop thief!"; but I heard nothing. I was alone in the alley. No one had seen me. The bread was a pound loaf. I broke it in two and hid it inside my clothes.

With half a loaf in my pockets and the other half in my stomach, I walked home. On the way I met a dog. I broke off a tiny piece of bread and threw it to him, because I did not want my luck to change. I did not beg anymore that day, for it is not true that it is easier to beg than to work, as some people say.

The sun finally came out; so I dragged my mattress from the cave and beat it with a stick. Then having filled the pail that "sack of bones" used to water his horse, I washed myself. There had been no soap in Naples for a long time now; and the land of the dirty had spread as had the land of the hungry. It is true that the poor of Naples always are dirty; for even if you have an extra shirt or a dress to wear while the other one is being washed and dried, you live among filth, and no matter how hard you try, the dirt will find a resting place upon you.

In the evening I walked down to the square. With surprise I noted on the faces of many of the other children that for them, this had not been a good day. A little boy whom I passed was crying; the sight of him annoyed me.

I saw Anna sitting with her brother on a curb. "Why aren't you at home?" I asked. "It is cold and late for a girl."

Anna looked up at me and smiled. "Guido, have you any bread?"

"No," I answered belligerently. I was glad that it was dark, for I was certain that could she see my face, she would know that I had lied.

"My aunt is sick. She is in bed."

"Then you ought to be at home!" I shouted at her.

I had not expected it, but the girl got up meekly, and taking her younger brother by the hand, started in the direction of the dark street on which she lived. I told myself to run after her and give her some of the bread that I had in my pockets; but I remained standing where I was.

"Good night, Anna," I called.

From across the piazza, her voice came, "Good night, Guido."

I had entered the square so happy and now I was miserable. 'Tomorrow I shall be unlucky,' I thought and walked homeward without talking to anyone. When I lay down on my mattress, I divided the remainder of the bread into three pieces: one I would eat tonight, as soon as I was warm; the other I would keep for the morning; and the third, I would give to Anna, as soon as I saw her.

Guido's Story

4

SMALL CHILDREN often speak of themselves as if
their souls could leave their small bodies, to stand
apart from them. "Luigi is crying," a little boy will
say and turn a tear-stained face towards his mother
for comfort. Almost all children in time start to
say, "I am crying" and "I want"; but there are a few
who never learn to do it — perhaps, because they
do not want to.

This is Guido's story . . . my story . . . No,
not mine, for Guido and I are not quite alike, although we are the same person. When the German
officer threw the money among the children, I
wanted to join in the fight for it; it was Guido who
did not want to. I can laugh at Guido; but I also
can curse him, for I want to be like the others. I
don't want to stand apart and watch myself

— at least, not all the time: not when I am sad, not when I am crying. Let me explain what I mean by telling you about certain things that happened to me before I came to Naples.

"Guido!" I looked up at the house. It was my aunt calling. "Guido!"

Every shutter and door in the house was closed because of the noonday heat, so that it looked as if no one lived there. My aunt was standing outside the back door. I knew why she was calling me. My mother was dying inside that house, and I was expected to come and sit at her bedside. I hesitated, I did not want to go, although I knew that I would. I could see the dark room, the bed, and my mother's face on the pillow. Her face was yellow like the images of the saints in their niches in the church. I could see myself sitting on the chair beside the bed, ten years old and crying: crying for the woman who lay so still, and was not my mother because I was afraid of her. This was what I saw as I sat on the stone fence below the house; and tears started to spring from my eyes.

"Guido!"

Slowly I rose and walked to the house. When I came near enough for my aunt to start scolding me I bent my head and hunched my shoulders. My aunt said nothing, she looked away from me as if she were ashamed.

"Your mother is dead." My aunt started to cry.

I stood still. I did not cry, for I had wept so much since my mother had first complained of the pains in her stomach that I seemed to have no tears left. 'I shall never have to sit beside her again,' I thought.

"A bad child . . ."
It was two weeks after my mother's funeral. My aunt was talking in a low tone to one of her neighbors.
"He cares about nobody. He talks to no one."
Twice I coughed so my aunt would know I was sitting outside the door; but then I realized that she wanted me to hear what she was saying. Either she had grown tired of speaking to me directly, or she thought that I could be shamed into better behavior more readily than I could be nagged. What my aunt said was true, I almost never spoke to anyone; my sorrow had grown inward and lamed my tongue.
"He can go a whole day without saying a word."
My aunt repeated the accusation, as if it were the worst crime one could commit; and maybe in her eyes, it was, for she talked so much that even when she was silent her hands would move, as if she were speaking.
My aunt had had eight children; six of them were living. Four were older than myself and two younger. She screamed at my cousins one minute and kissed them the next. She was always in movement: cooking, washing, cleaning; she reminded

me of a hen with a brood of chickens. I had often thought that we ought to tie a stone to one of her legs, as we did to the mother hens to prevent them from running too far away from their chicks. At night, when my uncle was asleep — for he was a hard-working man — she would drop to her knees in the corner, in front of the picture of the Blessed Mother; not to pray — no, to talk to Her! I have heard my aunt repeat the gossip of the village or complain about a neighbor, while she knelt, with hands clasped in front of her, gazing up at the Madonna.

'Yes,' I thought as I looked up at the dark sky, 'my aunt does not like silence. And it must be the worst of my crimes.' I smiled, for I was remembering something my mother had told me: "Your Aunt Antonia will live forever. God will be afraid of taking her to Paradise for fear she would talk him to death; and the devil won't have her." There had not been any very deep affection between the two sisters; but my mother had been the less cruel of the two, for she knew of her lack of love, while my Aunt Antonia did not, as she could never admit that she did not care for a sister.

My aunt had raised her voice, and without thinking, I turned to see her face in the light of the candle. "His mother was a silent one, too," she said.

I almost laughed out loud. My mother had not been silent; she had just never taken her sister into her confidence, but this Antonia would not have understood, for she spoke intimately to almost everyone. "Antonia . . ." This was the first time I had thought of that name without putting "Aunt" before it.

I walked away from the house, down to the stone fence, where I had sat so often with my mother. The sweet smell of the herbs that grew next to the wall filled my nostrils. Long after, when I would pass a vegetable vender in Naples, and I would smell the basil and the origanum, thoughts of my mother came back to me.

That night I decided to leave my uncle's house; not because I was mistreated there, but because I did not belong. This I could not have explained to my aunt; for to her, a sister or a cousin was family, and family belonged together.

I had lived with my mother across the straits in Sicily, in the city of Messina. When my father had gone to fight in Abyssinia, I had been a very little boy. My aunt had asked my mother and me to come and live with her. My mother had refused politely, though I have heard her say jokingly that the Straits of Messina protected her from her sister.

Sickness had brought my mother home, for the farm that my uncle and aunt lived on had belonged to her parents; she had been born there.

"It is pretty, Guido," she said while we were sitting in the train; and then she repeated it. "It is pretty, Guido."

I was looking out of the window and counting

the tunnels that the train was passing through.

"But it is a jail, Guido . . . a jail." So bitter were my mother's words that I turned from the window. She was very pale. She had become so thin; and yet the thought that she was dying did not occur to me, for I was only nine years old.

"You must mind your aunt and uncle."

I nodded.

"Your aunt screams a lot. She is not very clever, but I think her heart isn't bad." My mother looked out of the window for a moment. The compartment was full of people and I was sitting very close to her. "She is greedy, though. Greedy for land like all peasants."

Again I nodded, though I did not understand what she was saying; but I seldom asked questions. I had grown used to my mother speaking to me not as one speaks to a child — not even as one speaks to a grownup — but as one speaks to oneself, when one is trying to comprehend something that is difficult to grasp.

"She will lie to you all the time. They all lie. It is part of their lives. They don't know when or why they lie."

I snuggled closer to my mother and whispered, "Who?"

My mother smiled, and I thought, 'She is already there, and we have only come halfway.'

"The women. The men, too; but mostly, the women: they always lie. They scare you with lies

and reward you with lies. Then, at last, they kill
you with them."

I saw a tear on my mother's cheek and I kissed
her. She hugged me. "Little Guido," she said very
softly.

My mother lived nearly a year after we came to
the farm. In the beginning, the mountain air
seemed to have been good for her. Together we often walked the mile and a half to the village of St.
Marco; but by the beginning of the summer
the heat bothered her too much, as later the cold
of the winter would. But during the autumn, she

would walk as far as the stone fence with me and there we would sit, while she told me of her childhood.

Her father had died when I had been so young that I had never seen him; but my grandmother had once come to visit us in Messina. She was still living, but she made her home in Bari with one of my aunts who had married a customs official. From my grandmother's single visit to Messina, I had only the memory of a little old woman dressed in black with very thin and cold fingers. It was strange to hear my mother speaking of my grandmother now as she had been when she was young. I mean young as my mother; for the child divides human life into three: children or near children, grownups, and old people.

"My mother was afraid of my father. He was so strong. *Duro* . . . like iron. And yet he died and she is still alive and well. And then she was ashamed, for she had given him no boy for the land. Three daughters, but no boys. The land would go to sons-in-law: that was what embittered his life. A daughter-in-law is like a new cow in the stable but a son-in-law is a new *padrone:* he owns the land and has no memories of the beatings you have given him to make him respect you, when you are old. That was why he married Antonia to Giuseppi, because Giuseppi was weak. My father wanted to be the *padrone* till the day he died. He thought that he was going to live to be a hundred;

but he didn't. One day he lifted a sack into a cart and then he fell down. He was dead and he was only fifty-six."

This was the way my mother talked to me on those short autumn afternoons. Sometimes I listened and sometimes I didn't; somehow I knew that she only wanted me near her. I wasn't alone her child, her son; I was her only companion, the only one she wanted to talk to. She was so lonely and she knew that she was dying.

"They sold me."

It was a sunny October day; the kind that is as warm as summer and as clear as winter. I had been watching a lizard but at my mother's words, I turned to her and listened, for the thought of being sold like a slave has a curious appeal to a child.

"How old do you think I am, Guido?"

I gazed more intently at my mother's pinched face, which made her brown eyes appear so big. "You were twenty-seven at your last birthday. I remember, mother: twenty-seven." Was twenty-seven young or old? I asked myself; and then decided that it must be young.

"When I was married, I was only fifteen. I was fourteen when I was engaged."

These were almost children's years: fourteen was and fifteen, wasn't that more of a child's age than a grownup's?

"Father," I began, "was he also fifteen?"

My mother laughed and I realized that I had been foolish, and I turned to look at the lizard again.

"He was thirty-five when we were engaged and thirty-six when we were married."

Her statement did not shock me, for the grown-ups' concept of age difference is not understood by children, who always want to be older than they are.

"Was he . . ." I hesitated. "Was he nice?" I blurted. Somewhere deep in my memory there was a man in a soldier's uniform, who was holding me on his lap.

"He was nice," she said gently. "It was not his fault. It was my father . . . and my mother, too. You see, your father was willing to marry me without any dowry; then they wouldn't have to divide the land, give away any of the precious dry, goat land. Your father was a lieutenant. It was a great match. Everyone was satisfied . . . And I was only a child, who didn't know any better . . . And *he* was happy, for once *he* was happy."

I knew when my mother said "he," she meant my grandfather. Most of the time she spoke of her father this way: bitterly; but sometimes, I think that she felt love for him — or at least understanding. He must have been very strong; and her words "*duro* like iron" probably describe him best. Her mother, she seldom talked about. Yet this is not true, she mentioned her often; it was only that she never said anything that you would remember.

I wanted to make "Guido's story" short. My mother, my uncle and aunt, and the village of St. Marco do not belong to my tale . . .

And yet they do. For a tale is like a spider's web, with all the fine threads close together at the center spreading out farther and farther, until only four or five threads, each attached to a different branch — like poles — hold the whole web in place.

My mother died in the spring, and in the summer I ran away; it was the summer of 1941. I was eleven years old then. That was my age, but it was not Guido's; he was much older . . . I had kissed my mother and wept for her, but it was Guido who had listened to her and tried to understand.

When I left the farm, I stole for the first time. The money I took was my own. My mother had given me twenty-five *lire* a few weeks before she died; and my aunt had taken it away from me after the funeral. I am not blaming my aunt, for what would a child do with twenty-five *lire?* My aunt had said that she would keep it for me. The night I left, I took twenty-five *lire* from the box that stood behind the Madonna in the kitchen. There was more than twice that much money in the box; but I only took twenty-five *lire.*

I remember how I walked along the road that night, watching the shadows, especially of the gnarled olive trees; but I was not really afraid of the darkness, not as my cousins were. My mother had not been afraid and she had told me that the spirits that walked in the night were inside the people who saw them; and the only reason for being cautious in the dark was so that you would not fall.

It was not I, but Guido who brought me to Naples. Surely, I would have been caught and returned to my aunt's house. I would not have been clever enough to get the idea of the ticket and the piece of paper with the address. I might have cried, not smiled, when the man at the railroad station asked me where I was going.

"To my uncle's and aunt's; they live in Naples."
I slipped the little piece of paper on which, a few
minutes before, I had written the name of my uncle.
Under it, I had printed the street and number of
the apartment where I had lived with my mother
in Messina; but for the town, I had written in big
block letters: N A P L E S.

The man who sold the tickets looked at the paper,
and then at me.

"My uncle will meet me at the station," I said
and put a ten *lire* bill down on the counter.

The man grunted, but he sold me the ticket. When I picked it up and scooped the change into my other hand, I forgot the slip of paper.

"Wait, boy!"

I wanted to run out of the station; but then the thought, 'You cannot walk to Naples,' made me stand still. This, too, had been Guido.

"Your address," the man said holding up the slip of paper, "you'd better keep it, in case your uncle isn't there."

"Thank you." I had the paper in my hand, but the man was not satisfied.

"Put it in your pocket and don't lose it," he ordered.

"Thank you," I said again, as I carefully folded my "uncle's" address, and slipped it into the pocket of my shirt.

Once in the train, I felt that I was safe, for it was overfilled and in the mass of people, I would not be noticed. No one punched my ticket; and when I left the big station in Naples, I threw it away.

The great square with its cafés and fountain in the center — though there came no water from its many spouts — was filled with people. It wasn't dark yet; but already I felt alone and afraid. I did not even know in which direction I ought to go.

Then I remembered what my mother had said to me, when I finally had guessed that she was dying. "Guido, you must be strong. You are all alone. Be strong like iron . . . like *he* was. But be kind, too; or you will wear yourself and others out. Don't be so strong that you will become lonesome. Don't forget that your mother loved you. I didn't know that. You see, Guido, love and strength are the only things that matter: the only two things one needs."

As I walked across the square to find a place to hide, a place to sleep, I said her first words aloud to myself: "Guido, you must be strong. You are all alone."

The Death of an Old Man

5

By the spring of 1943, not only the poor were hungry in Naples; and fear was like a shadow that no man escaped. Since the bombardment of December fifth, war was no longer a word, it was the world we lived in.

During a war, the death of one man — especially an old man — seems hardly worth mentioning. Old "sack of bones" was not alone old, he was also poor; and if he had any family — brother or sisters — he never had mentioned them to anyone. I believe that in all of Naples only two people missed him after he was gone. But I was one of them, so I will tell you about his death.

After the big bombardment, old "sack of bones" worked almost everyday in the harbor, cleaning up the rubble. One day in April, he asked me to go along with him.

"I am old, Guido. It is the horse they want and

the cart, not me. You can come and help me."
Walking along beside the cart, the old man kept
complaining that the work was too hard for
the horse. "Guido, a horse belongs to the country.
It is not meant for the streets of a town. It wants
grass like the rest of us want spaghetti."

I nodded, thinking that none of us was made for
the city, for this world of cement and stone. This
was the first time that the idea of leaving Naples
struck me, and I expressed my wish aloud. "Why
don't you go into the country, too?" I added.

The old man spat on the ground. "The country,"
he mumbled. "In the country, no one leaves you
alone. They all know about you. The women
can shout for miles to each other. And then, one
would be in the way; there not being enough land."

'So he does come from the country,' I thought
eagerly. 'And somewhere there is a farm so small
that it could not be shared.' I wanted to know
more; and I said without looking up at him, "But
for the horse, it would be fine."

I was certain that "sack of bones" was watching me for some sign that I might be making fun
of him; and I kept my gaze on the wooden spokes
of the big wheel.

"For the horse, yes," he said, "for a horse is not
a man. It does not hurt anyone. It is not like a dog:
dogs are like men; they don't know when to die.
They bite and live off each other. A horse eats
grass, and when there is no more grass, it lays

down and dies. It is good, like God dying on the Cross . . . Men, they will eat each other. They are sacks of bones that the devil has blown life into."

I did not laugh, for the old man spoke without bitterness. I looked up at him, so he could judge from my glance that I was in earnest. "What about Father Pietro . . . and you? Was it the devil who blew life into you, as well?"

We were near the harbor, and beyond we could see the back of the sea stretching all the way to its meeting place with the sky; and I thought, 'The sea does not change. It must have looked like that when old "Sack of bones" was a child, too.'

"Father Pietro thinks that everyone is born good . . . No, he thinks that they are still good, even when their hatred and their evil are visible like sores on their faces . . . He makes himself blind, so that he can see, the way saints do."

I was waiting for the old man to answer the rest of my question. "But you?"

"Me?" He looked away for a moment; then when his eyes again met mine, he smiled timidly, as a child who is afraid does. "I know that you call me: 'old sack of bones.' And I know you laugh at me. It doesn't matter." He paused and then said slowly, "It doesn't matter now . . . But before, it did . . . I don't know what man is; but if he is not evil, then it is hard to bear. I am an old man, Guido, soon it will be all over." He pulled on the reins and stopped the horse. "It would be too terrible, if no one cared. All the suffering, Guido. You . . . the other children: all of them." He nodded behind him, towards the city. "They must be evil and created by evil. If that isn't true, it would be too terrible."

The old man repeated the words, "too terrible"; then he smiled as a person does when he is about to tell a secret. "Don Pietro, the priest, thinks God is there and that is why he can stand the suffering. I . . . I think the devil is there. That is the only thing that I believe in: that the devil . . . that the devil lives." As he said these last words, he bowed his head.

"Sack of bones" slackened the reins and the horse understood that the moment for resting had come to an end, and walked on. I did not understand the old man, for though I was hungry and poor, I did not think of my life as "too terrible."

Just as we came to the pier where we were to work, I asked, "You mean that if it was nobody's fault then . . ." I hesitated and started over again, "You mean if nobody was to blame, then it would be too terrible?"

The old man no longer wanted to talk. He shook his head. But I do not think he wanted to tell me that I was wrong. No, he was shaking his head at the world: at Naples, at Rome, at Messina, and all the countries that lay beyond the sea.

It was nearly noon, when I saw the flies on the horizon — except that they were not flies. They were airplanes that in the distance looked like flies. There were four of them. They were flying low over the water.

"They are two-motored bombers!" one of the men shouted. There were more than twenty of us working together; and somehow at the same moment, we all realized why the planes were there, and we ran to hide behind a wall.

I looked at the faces about me: some were white with fear, but others were calm as if they did not care what happened. 'The old man,' I thought, 'where is he?' I had been crouching; now I stood up.

"Sack of bones" wasn't there! I ran out from behind the wall.

The old man was standing beside his mare, one hand caressing her neck, and the other holding her bridle. I heard the engines of the planes. They were circling the harbor. Their target was a German ship, lying in the middle of the great basin. I stood motionless and watched them. I had forgotten the old man; I had even forgotten myself.

As the planes approached the ship, the bombs fell from their bellies. I knew they were bombs, though from the distance they did not look dangerous, as if they were only little black pebbles that could hurt no one.

The explosions came almost as a surprise, and I bent down as the noise deafened me. The ship had been hit; a great cloud of smoke was coming from it.

Three of the planes flew out towards the sea again, but the fourth changed its course, and flew straight towards us. I would have run back to the wall; but it was already too late. The plane dropped no bombs but it was shooting at the pier with its machine guns. It was flying so low that its propellers made the dust which covered the ground raise itself in clouds.

I had been lying down with my hands over my head. Now there was silence and I very slowly looked up. The plane was banking, heading out toward the sea. I hadn't been hit. Nothing had happened to me. I stood up and started to laugh. The men, as they came out from behind the wall, laughed, too. Twenty people laughing, and beyond in the harbor, the German ship was burning.

As if all of us at the same moment had realized that our laughter was meaningless, we stopped. I turned to look at the old man; the thought that he or the horse could have been hurt had not occurred to me.

The horse was lying down; but for a second my attention was attracted by the cart that was still standing behind the animal. We had been loading into it pieces of wall from the destroyed warehouses.

The mare's hind legs were still moving, as if she were trying to get up. "Sack of bones" lay outstretched near her head; and I thought he was trying to comfort her; but when I stepped closer, I saw the hole in his back from the bullet.

Four men carried him to the wall and lay him down. He was dead. Then I saw one of the men take from his pocket a jack-knife. He opened it and started walking towards the mare.

"No!" I screamed.

The man turned; his face was almost distorted by his fury. He screamed at me. "Look, boy! Look!"

Although the horse had been hit by several bullets, she was not dead. The one of her eyes that I could see was turned in such fear and pain that it appeared all white.

"Forgive me! I'm sorry!" I cried. I ran down the pier, away from the harbor, as if I were being pursued by fear itself.

I did not stop running before I was again in the narrow streets of the city, where the walls of the buildings locked from view the harbor and the blue sea.

Perhaps because I had been talking with "sack of bones" about Don Pietro, the thought of telling the priest what had happened occurred to me. I was breathless when I entered the church; and before I dipped my hand into the Holy Water next

to the entrance, I stood still and waited for my heart to stop throbbing in my ears.

I found the confession box empty. I stepped back wondering where I could look for the priest.

"What do you want, boy?"

I jumped, for in the semi-darkness I had not noticed Father Carlo.

"I want to speak to the old man," I said and glanced up at the youngest priest. I do not know why, but suddenly I hated Father Carlo more than I feared him.

"The old man? About whom are you talking?"

I should not have said "*il vecchio*," but Don Pietro. I knew this; but Father Carlo's ignorance was a pretense, for I had heard him many times call Father Pietro, "the old man"; and he had said it in a tone of contempt.

"Father Pietro," I mumbled. "I want to talk with Father Pietro."

To my amazement, the priest crossed himself.

"Father Pietro . . ." I repeated.

"Father Pietro is dead."

I shook my head and a voice within me said, 'No, it isn't true!'

"He died last night in his sleep."

"No!" I exclaimed aloud. "No, it isn't true!"

For a moment, I thought the priest was smiling, but maybe I was mistaken. "You shan't get his bread from him, anymore."

Instantly, I forgot all the times I had come to the

church to beg bread, and I believed no worse lie could ever be told about me, no greater injustice ever be done. The anger within me grew until I was filled with it. "And you are glad!" I pointed my finger at Don Carlo. "You are glad! Now you will eat it!"

The pain from the priest's blow, when he struck my cheek, did not still my rage. "You hated him! You hated him! It is a sin!" I ran towards the portal of the church; then I turned to look back at the motionless figure, whose features were dimmed by the darkness. "You hated him! You killed him! It is a mortal sin!" I shouted at Father Carlo.

When I came out into the sunlight, I was still crying; but all my hatred was gone.

"They were old men," I said to myself and then repeated the words, for they made the terrible fact of their dying more bearable.

6

"He's DIRTY, Mama." The little boy looked at me and then at his mother, who was standing at the kitchen table, slicing a piece of bread for me from a large country loaf.

"He is poor," the mother explained and she smiled towards me.

I was looking at the boy and thinking, 'And so would you be, if you lived as I do.'

"He is dirty," he repeated and glanced at his own hands. The mother gave me the bread and frowned at her son; but a second later, she was stroking his hair.

"Would you like some wine?" I nodded for my mouth was too full of bread for me to talk. She poured a large glass of wine from a half empty bottle. I drank it greedily for I was thirsty; but it was very sour and I must have made a grimace as I swallowed it.

"Is it too sour?" The woman was nervous, and when I didn't reply at once, she said hurriedly, "I thought it was all right. We use it for cooking."

I smiled, for I had noticed that she had stood long looking at the shelf, before she decided which of the several bottles to pour from.

My glance was on the bread. "Would you like another slice?" she asked.

"Yes, Signora," I responded and then added, "I have not eaten all day." This was not a lie, and I could truthfully have added that I had not eaten yesterday, as well; but I was afraid she would not believe me. This time she gave me a larger piece than before and poured a glass of wine from a different bottle without asking me.

"Why doesn't your mother wash you?" The little boy looked at me so seriously that I was amused.

"Because I have no mama."

The child was bewildered. He came from a different world and he was only four years old. "Everybody has a mama. Why doesn't yours wash you?"

I blushed and said again, "I have no mama."

"Then why doesn't your Anna wash you?"

I grinned for the mentioning of that name made me think of my friend Anna, and certainly she was much dirtier than I was.

"Anna is our cook. She washes him sometimes. He thinks that everyone has an Anna at home." The lady laughed and the little boy was annoyed, for he probably realized that he had said something stupid.

"Why don't you wash him, Mama?"

I wished that I was well out of the house, for now the mother was laughing very loudly. When she saw my discomfort, she said softly, "Maybe I shall, Giorgio." I took a step backwards, prepared to run.

"Don't be afraid. You just looked so funny."

I turned away from both of them; I was angry, especially at the mother.

"How old are you?"

"Twelve," I replied and dried my nose with my hand.

"He doesn't use his handkerchief. He doesn't use his handkerchief!" Little Giorgio sang joyously."

"And what is your name?"

"Guido."

"Guido," the woman repeated slowly; then paused and declared that it was a good name.

I had never thought that a name could be good or bad: a name was like a stone; it just was.

"Where do you live?"

"Down below," I said and pointed to the floor.

I was begging that afternoon in Vomero, that district that was on top of the hill, high above our cave.

I knew three good houses in Vomero, where I was seldom refused. This was the third one, for though I had never before heard her name, I knew the cook; she was very generous with the food of her mistress. I had already been at the two other houses: one had been closed up, the owners had left Naples; in the other, I had received ten *lire* from the count, himself. If I had not been in Vomero, I would not have gone to the third place; but in this district there are only a few stores, and if I had tried to enter any of them, I might have been called a thief.

The count was a strange man, who always wore a yellow dressing gown that came all the way down to his feet like the robe of a priest. The first time I came to his house, his servant had not only thrown me out but boxed my ears as well. Once outside the house, I had spat at it. If I had not been so furious, I probably would have run away when the old man called me.

"Why do you spit on my house, little scoundrel?" The old man had stuck his head out of the window on the second floor. It had been winter and he had worn a red flannel scarf around his neck. "Come up here." He had waved his hand at me, drawn in his head, and closed the window.

My first thought had been to run away; my second, to spit on the house again, and then walk slowly down the street, to show that I was not afraid. But I had done neither, I had waited obediently, until the servant who had boxed my ears opened the door; then I had taken a step backwards.

"My master wants to talk with you." As I had given no indication of whether I would follow him, he had added, "He won't hurt you."

Trying to look insolent, to hide that I was prepared to run, I had walked towards the door.

"Don't tell him that I hit you."

"Why shouldn't I?" I had answered, for I had not been as afraid of the servant as I had been of the old man with the scarf.

"I will give you fifty *centesimi,* if you don't." I had held out my hand and the servant had thrust a coin into it; then he had mumbled something so softly that I could not hear him.

'I will tell the old man,' I had thought to myself. 'I will tell him that I was beaten.'

But I had said nothing when I stood before the count, for the size of the room, the furniture, and the pictures hanging on the walls had made me dumb.

"Why did you spit at my house?"

I had muttered, "I am poor," and had tried to shrug my shoulders.

"The rich spit on the poor, and the poor spit on the rich, that is democracy."

I had not known the meaning of the word "democracy"; therefore, I had turned my eyes away from the old count. On the opposite wall had hung a large painting of a lady dressed in a gown of lace. When the old man had noticed what had attracted my attention, he had said, "That is a portrait of my grandmother."

Without thinking I had asked, "Is she dead?"

My question had made the old man laugh. "I am seventy-one."

My face had grown red because of my foolishness; and the count being a kind man had looked away so as not to embarrass me further.

"Are you an orphan?"

I had nodded and had been about to add my usual complaint, "My father died in Africa," but I had not wanted to say it in this beautiful hall.

"You may come once a week." The count had taken a purse from a large pocket in his gown and had given me a two *lire* piece. "Once a week, not oftener."

I had bowed and said thank you; and the old man had smiled at me. But a moment later, he had frowned. "I don't think that I should give you anything, for you are a little scoundrel. Now you can go."

Again I had bowed. I had turned, the door which the servant had closed behind me, had now been opened.

"Giacomo, the boy can come once a week."

The servant had smiled, as if the news he had just heard had pleased him; but when he had closed the door behind me, the smile had left.

'He has been listening at the door,' I had thought, 'but he couldn't hear.'

"I didn't tell," I had said aloud.

The servant had said nothing until I was again on the street, then he had called after me, "Remember, only once a week."

I had stood for a long time staring at the window, out of which the old man had stuck his head; I had wanted to stick my tongue out at Giacomo, but I hadn't dared. Then I had sworn to myself that I would never come back; yet I had come, for a hungry stomach argues well against pride.

Now that I have begun, I shall also tell you of the last time I saw the old count, when he gave me a ten *lire* piece.

As I have already said, the first house I visited that day had been closed up; and the people who lived there were gone. When I arrived at the count's, the servant met me at the door; but he would not let me enter. They were packing, he explained, there was no time for me. I was very hungry so I argued loudly, hoping that the count would hear me.

The door upstairs opened, and the count called down to ask what was the matter. I did not let the servant answer, quickly I shouted, "It is I, the little scoundrel!" The old man never called me by any other name.

"Come up," the count ordered. I grinned triumphantly at Giacomo, who scowled back at me.

To my surprise the count was dressed. The hall was half empty. I found myself looking for the painting of the lady in the lace gown. It was gone, but on the wall there was a lighter square, where it had hung.

"Well, little scoundrel, have you come to say good-bye?"

I nodded, though it was not true: I had come for my weekly two *lire*.

"They say that the captain is the last to leave the ship." The count looked around the almost bare room. "Now you know that it is not true."

'What is he talking about?' I asked myself silently. 'He is not a captain and Naples is not a ship.' Aloud, I said, "You are leaving?" I knew that my question was silly; but I thought that I ought to say something.

"Yes . . ." The old man paused; and I am sure that he was about to say "little scoundrel"; but he changed his mind, and asked me my name. I mumbled what it was, and he went on with what he had begun to explain, "Yes, Guido, I am leaving. I am old and I don't think I shall come back."

Then it was that he took out his purse and gave me the ten *lire* note. "Now you go. You are young." He patted me on the shoulder and repeated the words, as if being young now had more meaning than ever before.

At the front door, Giacomo met me. And then,

there happened something unexpected, like a miracle . . . No, not a miracle for it was not as important as that. Giacomo gave me five *lire!* Then when I wanted to thank him, he pushed me out of the door. Five *lire* to Giacomo was a lot of money, just as one *lira* was to me.

"Is it bad down there?"

I did not know what the lady was talking about, for my thoughts were still with the count and his servant.

"The big bombardment, was it very terrible?"

"Yes," I replied, for it had been horrible. This had been the first bombardment in which any part of Naples but the harbor had been hit; and bombs had fallen in many sections of the city. My own district had not suffered. After the attack was over, I had gone down to one of the areas that had been hardest hit; there I had seen the soldiers dragging the dead and wounded out of the ruins.

"It frightens me."

The lady's admission of fear delighted me; as if it were a kind of revenge. But within a few moments, I was ashamed, and I said, "It frightens everyone, Signora."

"I don't know why, but my assertion seemed to disappoint her. *"Che miseria! . . .* What misery!" she said unhappily.

I noticed Giorgio. He was looking at his mother with the same anxiety that I had seen so often in the faces of poor children. His mother's sadness was about to make him cry. 'He doesn't understand what she is talking about,' I thought, 'but he senses her despair. That is the way little ones are, the troubles of the parents make them unhappy, even though they do not know what they are all about.' I smiled at the child; but he grimaced back at me. He wanted his mother to laugh.

"I had better go," I said. "I want to get back before it gets dark."

The woman bit her lip and looked down at the child. "I am all alone. Anna has gone to visit her sister, and my husband is in Rome."

I knew that she wanted me to stay because she was frightened. She offered me another piece of bread and even gave me a slice of salami.

"Isn't Anna coming soon?" I asked.

"She promised to come back before it was dark." The signora looked at me pleadingly; what she wanted to say was: 'Stay until then,' but she did not dare.

The reason that I did not want to stay was that I was afraid of the police in Vomero. They were stricter than in the rest of Naples; and I knew that they picked up beggar children whom they found on the streets at night and sent them to the orphanages. Just as I was about to explain this to the lady, there was a long howling sound. It came from somewhere behind the house. When the sirens sounded the third time, Giorgio began to cry.

'It comes from the funicula station,' I thought, as if it were important for me to know of its exact location.

"Sit down. You must stay."

The woman's eyes appeared very large. 'It must be fear,' I thought, as I sat down across from her and the child, who was now whimpering almost silently.

7

"They won't bomb here . . . I mean not Vomero."

The signora, who had folded her hands as if she were praying, attempted to smile. I noted that her lips were thin, not full as my mother's had been.

"You don't think so?" she asked timidly.

"No," I answered. "It will be the harbor again, or maybe Pozzuoli, or some factory." And I thought to myself, though I did not say it out loud, 'And close to the harbor or near the factories live only poor people.'

"Still . . . They could by mistake . . ." she whispered, and drew in her lower lip and began to bite it gently.

"They could," I agreed, and I looked out of the kitchen window. It was twilight. While I stood there, I realized that it would be better if we were in the corridor, where there were no windows. "We'd better sit in the hall," I said.

The woman quickly put little Giorgio, who had been sitting on her lap, down. She was obeying me as if I were a grownup; and I was amazed.

In the hall, there were two chairs and a table. I turned on the light; there was still electricity. "Have you any candles?" I asked.

She responded by going at once to the kitchen to fetch them. The little boy, who was frightened, followed her. When she came back, I said hesitantly, "I will go and close the shutters. Sometimes the glass breaks, that is why we should sit in the hall."

"Thank you," she whispered.

First I went to the kitchen and closed both the inner and the outer shutters. From the kitchen a door led to the dining room, and I paused before I opened it. The apartment of the signora was not as elegant as the count's house. There were seven rooms. One was very small, and I guessed that it must be the cook's room. The last room I entered was Giorgio's. His bed was like a large cradle, and had a kind of awning above it. The material was light blue and so fine that you could see through it; it was held aloft by four painted poles. "You are a beggar boy," I said aloud; and then as if the sound of my own voice enchanted me, I repeated, "You are a beggar boy, Guido . . . A beggar boy."

Just as I was leaving the room, I noticed a teddy-bear. I decided to take it to the boy. Next to the bed was a little table on which were some picture books; I picked four of them. I, too, had had a stuffed animal when I had been little. I had had a toy dog, when I lived with my mother in Messina; but Giorgio's teddybear was much larger.

When I returned to the hall, the signora was sitting with Giorgio on her lap; the child had stopped crying. I handed him the teddybear and put the books down on the table. The mother smiled at me approvingly.

"Would you like some cognac, Guido?"

I almost said yes; but then I recalled that I had once tasted cognac and hadn't liked it, so I refused; but I thanked her, because I was only twelve years old and it was a compliment to offer me cognac.

For a while we sat in silence, listening for the sound of the airplane motors. I was thinking of the old count, wondering where he was going. Giacomo, the servant, had once told me that the count owned three very large estates and that more than a hundred families lived on each of them. Then when he had told me about the estates, I had thought the servant exaggerated in order to impress me; but now I was not sure. And I thought to myself, 'The count has so much land that he does not need to live on it, and others have so little that they cannot. But he will go back to the land . . .' Now his words came back to me: "Guido, you know now that it is not true, that the captain stays with his ship." When he had spoken to me, I had not understood him; but now as I waited for the approach of the planes, I did; and I almost said out loud, 'It was because of shame that he said that. It made him feel better, and that is why he asked me my name.'

I often talked silently to myself, when there was something I did not understand. I would ask and Guido would answer. That at least is the way I felt it was, though, naturally, I knew that I was only one person. 'The count doesn't realize that we don't care whether he leaves or not. He does not know us, he only thinks that he does.'

"I lighted a candle this morning."

It was the signora speaking, but I had been so busy conversing with myself that I now looked confused.

"It was lucky, wasn't it? I mean, I couldn't have known that there would be an air-raid."

Sometimes anger comes upon one without warning, as a wave on a smooth sea; and it enters one's chest and chokes one. "My mother lighted a candle for my father every Sunday, yet my father died in Africa!"

The lady bowed her head and mumbled that she was sorry.

"One should never tell when one has lighted a candle, it brings bad luck."

The signora sighed so deeply at my words, that she almost moaned.

"It is always good to light a candle," I said softly, not caring that I was contradicting myself, for my anger had disappeared and now I pitied her. 'She is foolish,' I thought. 'She does not know God, as Father Pietro or old "sack of bones" did.'

"We should be good to each other, shouldn't we, Guido?"

"Yes," I answered, but I could not help thinking, 'She is afraid and that is the voice of fear.'

"I pray for everyone." The woman bent her head to kiss her child who was sitting half asleep in her lap.

'How could she?' I thought. 'How could she pray for everyone, for people whom she did not know? You prayed for those you loved — the other was like praying for no one. It is just telling Our Lady how good you are. It is a bribe. A bribe because she is afraid.'

"We are all God's children, you and little Giorgio." I said nothing and she clutched the child so tightly that he started to cry. "But the poor are sacred to Him."

Within me a voice screamed, 'What do you know of the poor?' And because the voice was so angry, I said nothing out loud.

The signora and I heard the planes at the same time, and she cried out, "*Madre mia . . .*" She threw up her hands and almost let the boy fall from her lap. I thought of my own mother and how well she had faced death; but then we were poor, and that may be why we do not fear death so much, for we live with it.

In a piteously sobbing voice, Giorgio cried out, "Anna! Why isn't Anna here? I want Anna!"

"I shouldn't have let her go, today. I knew it this morning," the mother wailed.

My glance fell upon the picture books that I brought from Giorgio's room. I took the one lying on top and gave it to the signora, and commanded, "Read it to him."

The woman took the book and opened it. At that moment we heard the first explosions. I listened intently, the noise came from the harbor. The signora dropped the book and started to weep; through her tears, she was muttering a prayer, a plea to God.

The child looked wildly about the room calling the cook, "Anna! Anna!" While my ears were listening to the explosions, trying to guess which part of the city was being hit, I thought, 'Yes, she takes care of him. The cook is in a way his mother.' Because of these thoughts, little Giorgio became dear to me, as if he really were my brother.

"Come here." I lifted the child from the lap of the signora and placed him on my own; then I grinned at him and wrinkled my nose. "Don't be frightened."

Giorgio tried to dry his tears with the back of his

hands, and he smeared them all over his little face. He looked so funny that I laughed. My laughter reassured him and he tried to smile.

"What book should I read: this one?"

He shook his head vigorously. He pointed to one of the other books on the table.

" 'Once upon a time, there were three little chickens: a black one, a white one, and a red one . . .' " I paused, for I heard an explosion not far away. The windows rattled and one could feel the house shake. "It is down below in my district." I thought of my friend Anna and her brother.

"Read on." It was not Giorgio but his mother.

I continued reading about the three little chickens. The black one was the naughty one. I had never read a book like that before, and I thought it very silly; yet I knew that I, too, was less frightened because I was reading.

When I finished reading the third book — they were very short, being mostly pictures — the raid was over. The noise of the planes grew soft as they flew away; and the anti-aircraft-guns stopped firing.

"You read so well!" the signora spoke calmly now. Giorgio slipped from my lap and sat down on his mother's.

The all-clear came through the doors of the hall. "It sounds so different," the lady said. I nodded in agreement, for to me, too, the sound of the all-clear, though it was the same as the warning of an on-coming air-raid, sounded very different.

The signora opened the door to the kitchen. "You were right, they did not hit Vomero."

I looked up at her and thought, 'She, too, is different now . . . like the siren.'

"I must go." I glanced around the hall and into the kitchen, wondering what it was that I was seeking.

"Won't you stay the night? You could sleep here." She cleared her throat. "I mean, if you wanted to . . ."

She was looking at me apprehensively, and I knew that she now wanted me to leave as much as she had wanted me to stay before.

"I think my district was hit."

"But you have no family."

"I have friends!" I exclaimed and walked quickly to the front door of the apartment.

"Make him stay. I like him!"

I had forgotten the boy; I had not even noticed him standing next to his mother, holding onto her skirt.

"I have to go home; but I will come and visit you again." I smiled at Giorgio and touched his cheek, for I was lying.

"Come again! Come again!" Giorgio exclaimed.

"Yes, you must come again." The mother had grabbed the child's words as if they were a sweet, and she were the same age as Giorgio. "Come again."

I had my hand on the door to the apartment

when she called me back. I knew she was going to give me money and that I could injure her by refusing it, and though this was what I wanted to do — hurt her — I stood still and waited.

The signora returned to the kitchen for her purse. She opened it and looked into it. The sight was so familiar to me. A thousand times, I had stood waiting like this and hoping that the person whose hand was rummaging through the purse would give me at least a *lira;* but this time I prayed instead that she would give me very little.

I almost laughed when she dropped the fifty *centesimi* into my hand. "Thank you, Signora. Thank you very much! *Grazie mille* . . . a thousand thanks!"

The woman's face flushed. I think she was going to speak, but I ran out of the door and down the stairs. When I reached the street, I started to laugh so loud that I startled myself. A moment later I was crying.

After the Raid

8

I T WAS the smell of dust from broken walls that I
noticed first when I came near my part of town,
that and the smell of smoke. But the smell of smoke
is a good smell, a comforting smell, while that of
dust feels sharp in your nose. The fine particles
enter your mouth with the air; they get between
your teeth and taste bitter.

Strange that anything so solid as a house can
tumble so quickly, that within minutes a building
in which people have lived for generations can be

a ruin; naked, with a past that you can only guess at. Dead . . . Dead like old "sack of bones." Dead without a future like old men and women who have no family to mourn for them.

Several of the houses near the piazza where we gathered had been hit. Children were ransacking the rubble. An old woman was trying to scare the children with a stick; but they were more amused than frightened by her. I recognized her, she had had a tiny apartment in the building that now all lay beneath her feet like a heap of rubbish.

She was looking for something. In her one hand she carried a broken pitcher, while with the other she tried to push aside heavy pieces of broken timber . . . All the while, she was calling a name.

One of the boys — he was one of the older ones and he had parents, so that he was not badly off — threw a stone at the woman. It fell against her back. It was not a large stone and it hit her almost without force; yet she sat down among the rubble and started to wail. She let the pitcher slip from her hand and it broke into several pieces.

I was on my way to look for Anna at her aunt's house; but I could not drag my attention away from the weeping old woman.

"What is the matter, Signora?"

She drew her hands away from her face to look at me; then impulsively she raised them again and let her head sink into her arms.

"You were looking for someone . . . Who is it?"

I waited but no answer came. A piece of the pitcher lay next to my foot, I bent down and picked it up. It had been very beautiful once; the kind of pitcher that one might be given by an aunt or an uncle on the day of one's marriage. The kind which was never used; and therefore, valued very highly among the poor, for they have so few things that need not be used.

"Tell me whom you were looking for and I will help you."

Again the woman looked at me. This time she opened her mouth and tried to smile: it was a foolish smile; a smile beyond fear, but not beyond pain.

"My cat," she finally muttered. Tears came into the corners of her eyes; two big tears that stayed there as if they were the last tears her eyes possessed. Not far from me, I heard someone crying the name of a child with a hopelessness that only knowledge can give.

"I am sorry," she cried. "I am sorry!"

I threw down the piece of porcelain and heard it break against a stone.

Hiding her face again, she wept. "It was all I had!"

My contempt became pity. "You will find it . . . I am sure you will . . . It has probably just run away because it was frightened by the noise."

I waited but she did not raise her head again. I could hear her wailing behind me as I walked away.

The boy who had thrown the stone was laughing. He had found a metal pot and was drumming on it with two sticks.

I don't know why I knew that Anna's house had been hit; but I felt certain of it long before I saw the gaping hole in the row of houses in her street. Soldiers were working among the ruins and I was ordered away, when I approached; so I joined a group of people on the sidewalk.

"They have found someone!" the man standing next to me shouted. I looked up at him. He was not from our district; he was too well dressed.

"It's a woman . . . Look!"

All we saw was a limp figure in a torn black dress.

"There must be more under the rubble," the voice next to me sounded so eager.

"Anna . . ." I whispered.

"God, there must be hundreds of dead or thousands." Now the man was looking at me, speaking to me directly.

Silently, I glanced up at him. He looked away; then he crossed himself. Only now he had remembered to do it. I continued to stare at him; he walked away and stood among another group of spectators.

I could not stay there, watching and waiting. I imagined Anna's body beneath the crumbled walls. It would be motionless and lifeless as that woman's

had been. Unconsciously, I crossed myself again; and it struck me that I was alive. This unexpected thought filled me with shame.

When I came to my cave, the little half door was open; and there was a flickering light from inside. Anna was sitting on my mattress and her brother was beside her. I did not call out but stood silently looking at them.

Along my way home, I had tried to tell myself that it was because I was alone that I cared so much what happened to her. I had passed a little child who was weeping and had wanted to stop and speak to him; but my will had not been my own and I had walked on. I had seen dozens of destroyed houses and had heard the survivors, as they crawled among the rubble, crying out names or calling in desperation: "Mama . . . Babbo . . . Nonno . . . Zia . . . Mother, father, grandfather, aunt . . ."

'She was like me,' I thought; then I had started to talk out loud to myself. "It isn't just death, not only that . . . Something else . . . Like the old woman with her cat; it was all she had." I had stood still and cocked my head, as if I really had been listening to someone speaking. "No, Guido. It is not like that . . . Not like the old woman with the cat." There had been a man sitting on the curb; I had noticed that he was staring at me; so I had hurried on.

Anna was drawing with a stick on the earth beside the mattress. As usual, her little brother was crying; and I marveled that so many tears could be in so small a body.

Anna did not look up until my shadow fell across them; then she spoke so softly that I could hardly hear her. "My aunt is dead."

I sat down between her and her brother; the little boy moved closer to me and stopped crying. Anna continued to draw. Carefully, as if it were something she had to do, she put one straight line next to another. I stuck out my foot and crossed her lines. She dropped the stick and turned towards me.

'She hasn't been crying,' I thought; but at that moment her eyes grew glassy. She did not try to dry her tears with her hands, as I would have done; but let them fall freely. 'They are like pearls,' I thought — somewhere I had read that once and not believed it, that tears could be like pearls; but in the candlelight, Anna's tears appeared that shiny and clean.

When Anna had started to cry, her brother had begun to wail. "Stop it," I said; but this made him cry all the more bitterly and I felt guilty as if I had hit him. "Stop and I shall buy you some bread."

He looked up at me to see whether I was in earnest; then he dried his eyes and nose with his dirty hands. To Anna, I said nothing, for I thought that her tears had to be shed just as some words have to be spoken.

As abruptly as she had begun to cry, so abruptly did she stop. She sighed and picked the stick up again; then she glared at it, as if she were surprised to find herself holding it, and threw it away.

"I was afraid that you were gone," she said.

"I have been at your house . . . I thought that you were dead."

"We were away. My aunt was alone. She was sick. She was lying in her room and — "

"There was an old woman who was crying for her cat," I interrupted Anna, for no reason except that I couldn't stop myself from talking.

"In our house?" Anna asked bewildered; then wrinkled her brow trying to think who it could have been.

"In another house, down by the piazza." I told her what had happened and how the woman's sorrow over the cat had angered me.

"But why had the boy thrown a stone at her?"

I had not thought of it until Anna asked the question; but now I found it as curious as she did. Most of us children would steal; we would throw a stone after another child if we were mad enough; but I could not remember ever seeing anyone cast a stone after an old woman. "Maybe he was scared," I suggested uncertainly. "I mean he was still scared after what had happened, and that was what made him do it."

"I don't know," Anna said. "But maybe . . ." She nodded towards her younger brother. "Mario is always crying; but during the bombardment, he didn't shed a tear. I think he was too scared to cry."

The little boy tried to smile. His head bobbed up and down to show that he had understood his sister and agreed with her. Anna could not help smiling. When the boy saw the smile, he started to laugh and said loudly as he pointed at me, "He is going to buy us bread!"

"You'll live with me," I said.

"Grazia . . . Thank you," Anna whispered even more softly than when she had told me of her aunt's death.

9

"I AM SORRY, Guido." The carpenter, the *padrone* of the cave, looked down at me sideways from his bench. Pursing his lips, he tried to express his regret silently, to show that it was not his fault.

I shrugged my shoulders. "I understand," I replied.

The carpenter was old and he could get no more wood. There was no reason for him to keep on paying rent for the cave. The new *padrone,* who had also bought the old man's tools, didn't want a stranger in the cave, for he and his family were going to live there, themselves. Their own home had

been destroyed a few days before in a bombardment.

"I am sorry," the old man repeated; then he
shook his head. "These are bad times, Guido."

I smiled, for the thought had come to me, that
this was how most misfortune befell one: by
chance!

"All you children have grownup eyes and children hearts . . . Even the tiny ones on their mothers' arms have the eyes of old people."

"Everyone is tired, so why shouldn't the children
be?" I argued; but to myself I said, 'He is wrong,
the old man. It is only he who is tired. Tired because he just wanted to grow old and now the war
won't let him.'

"You know, I never said anything about *them*
coming to live here." The carpenter motioned towards the doorway; just outside it, Anna and her
young brother were sitting on the ground.

I had long since explained to the carpenter that
Anna and Mario were sister and brother; and that
the aunt with whom they had been living had been
killed during a bombing raid.

"Didn't I believe you when you said you had to
take care of them?" The old man laughed, though
his lips did not form a smile.

He was making fun of me and I turned away from
him to look at that corner of the cave that I had always thought was my own. I had long daydreamed
about leaving the city; but this cave had kept me

from going, for I had feared giving up my home.
Suddenly I remembered little Giorgio's room in
Vomero. I closed my eyes and I saw that strange
bed with the little blue tent above it. 'Home,' I
thought bitterly, 'how can I call this a home?'

"I was thinking of going away anyway," I said
aloud.

"Where will you go?"

As if I had known the answer to the question before it was asked, I said, "To Rome." I had no
sooner spoken the words than I was amazed: Why
had I said Rome? When I had thought of leaving
the city, I had never had any exact place in mind;
but I had always thought of the country, where
there would be grass. Rome was a city like Naples;
why should I want to go there?

"Do you know anyone in Rome?" The old man's
forehead was wrinkled.

"I have an uncle there." Though my face was
very serious, inside I was laughing, for I realized
that the carpenter believed me. "He works for the
railroad," I added.

The old man nodded, as if to say, 'that is a good
steady job.'

Quickly I gave myself an aunt and cousins; then I
described Giorgio's mother's apartment in Vomero,
as if it belonged to my aunt and uncle. I know I
spoke convincingly, though all the while, I was
asking myself why I was inventing so many lies.

"You go to them, Guido."

And while I said, yes; for that tiny fraction of a moment, just long enough for one to blink one's eye, I, too, believed that I had an aunt and an uncle in Rome.

"Go alone, Guido. Don't take anyone with you. Your aunt and uncle won't like there being others along. You will get there faster alone."

As he spoke I realized that Mario had stopped crying. I knew now why he cried so much. He had stomach aches. I believe they came from not eating enough; Anna and I had them, too, though they didn't bother us so much.

"Oh, I shall go alone," I assured the carpenter.

"That's right, Guido." The old man's voice sounded so anxious as if it were of great importance to him that I should leave Anna and her younger brother behind; and if I had dared I would have asked him why.

"Does your uncle work in the freight yard?"

"Yes."

"I know that kind; they earn good money and a pension for their old age. They will have to help you, you being in the family; but they won't do anything for anyone else."

For a moment, I wanted to protest, for that was not the kind of "uncle" I had thought of, when I started lying.

"Here." Out of his pants pocket the old man brought a crumpled *lira* note. "Here, you take it. It will help you."

"Thank you," I said; then I recalled that once when old "sack of bones" hadn't been able to pay his rent, the carpenter had threatened to throw him and his horse out.

"When will the new *padrone* come?"

"Tomorrow. You will have to be out in the morning."

"I'll be gone," I said and put the *lira* in my pocket.

"Don't steal anything," the carpenter said breathlessly.

I was shocked. I had never thought of taking anything that was in the cave.

"I am sorry, Guido."

Slowly I raised my glance. There was remorse in his face; but if he regretted what he had said to me it was because he feared that he had given me an idea, that he now realized I had not had before.

"Do you want my mattress?" I asked.

The crafty smile that came to the old man's face made me hate him. "Guido, I will come tomorrow morning and buy it from you. I shall give you three *lire* for it."

'He thinks I will steal everything in the cave, and he is trying to buy me off with three *lire*,' I thought. Aloud I asked, "When will you come in the morning? I want to leave early."

"I shall come after Mass," the old man replied and, getting down from his bench, he patted my head. "I will give you three *lire*."

I followed the carpenter to the entrance of the cave. Anna looked up at us when we passed her on our way to the street, and the carpenter poked me in the ribs and whispered, "Go alone, don't take anyone with you."

I was trying to think of something clever to say; something that would arouse the old man's suspicions again, make him believe that I would steal everything in the cave; but he now seemed so miserable. He was bent forward as if he had to look at the ground in order to walk with even step.

"I'll be waiting for you in the morning. Don't worry, I shan't take anything."

"I know you won't, Guido," he exclaimed and put his arm around my shoulders. "I know you won't, but these are evil times, and I am old, and I had to sell them. The things haven't any value; it's the place he is buying: my rights to it; but if the tools weren't there, he could go to the police, and he wouldn't have to pay me." The words came quickly as if the carpenter feared that he would not say them at all, if he spoke slowly.

"I won't touch anything. And you needn't buy my mattress."

The old man stepped away from me in order to look at my face. He smiled simperingly. "You are a good boy, Guido. May Our Lady take care of you."

We parted and he started down the street; but he had not gone more than a few steps when he turned around, "Guido, do what your aunt and uncle tell you to do, then everything will be all right. All they want is obeying."

I nodded and waved good-bye. 'Why doesn't he sleep in the cave?' I asked myself and the answer came to me with certainty: 'Because he is afraid. He will be afraid until he dies.' And I felt sorry for him, for though he was an old man he was like Anna's little brother.

"Who is your uncle?" Anna asked, when I came back to the cave.

Laughingly, I said, "He is working in a railroad yard in Rome." I would have continued, told more lies about my imaginary uncle, but I noticed Anna's expression. "I have no uncle," I said. "I made it all up."

Anna frowned and turned away from me.

"But none of it's true," I persisted.

"Why did you say it then?"

I did not know myself, why I had made up the story, so I told still another lie: one that I knew would convince her that I was telling the truth.

"I had to say all that about my uncle to the carpenter, or he might have told the police that we had nowhere to go."

Anna sighed deeply and looked up at me admiringly. My explanation had satisfied her, for all the parentless children of Naples, all the little fishes, feared nothing more than the police and the orphanages to which the police took them. Some of the older children even paid grownups out of pathetic earnings as beggars, to pose as their fathers or mothers and protect them from the orphanages. I do not really know what these homes for parentless children were like, as no one truly knows what Hell is like; but I once spoke with a boy who had run away from one of them and he bore the marks from a beating on his back.

"I do have an uncle in Bari," I said, "but I don't know his address. Have you any relatives?"

Anna whispered, "Don't go to your uncle, please."

Her plea made me feel happy. "I shan't leave you," I promised; and I recalled the carpenter's warning. 'He would have left her,' I thought. 'And that is why he wanted me to do it. He wants the whole world to be like himself.'

"We shall stay together always!" I said loudly.

10

WHEN A human being is mortally wounded, he dies quickly; and even while he is dying, death takes possession of him and says: "He is mine."

A city does not die, for life even among the ruins will continue to deny its doom. Children will play, whose parents have been dead but a week; grownups will make new homes in the cellars of destroyed buildings. Even the rats with their hard little eyes have somewhere among the rubble naked little babes that they return to.

Still the smell of death is there; but the inhabitants do not recognize it, for they have grown used to it, as farmers grow accustomed to the heavy,

sweet smell of the orange blossoms. If you came
as a stranger to the city, things would fill you with
horror, that the people living there do not even
notice. You might even say, "This city is dying,"
and flee from it with fear; but your fear would not
have sprung from the ruins, not even from the smell
of death that comes from beneath them, but from
your memory, which was still filled with the life of
peace, of another world, of the dew of morning.
You would be as a horse who was led to a muddy
hole to drink; a horse who that very dawn had
drunk from a pure spring. The horse would turn
away; yet I have seen animals in Calabria during
the hot month of August swallow the moist earth
that weeks before had ceased to be a pool. Such
animals were the citizens of Naples in the beginning
of the summer of 1943.

"You will have to wash him and yourself, too.
You are both dirty."

Pleadingly Anna looked up at me; then she took
Mario by the hand and led him to the center of the
cave, where I had placed the bucket of water. The
bucket had belonged to "sack of bones"; he had
used it to water his horse. The water I had gotten
from the public faucet on the square. It was the
only place in the whole district where one could
get water. During the day there were long lines
of women and children with pails and pitchers waiting their turns. I had been there that morning be-

fore the sun rose; and although I did not have to wait, I was not the only one who had come so early.

"Take his clothes off," I ordered. "You can't wash him like that."

Anna, who had been wetting her hands in the bucket and then rubbing Mario's face and arms gently as if she were merely trying to moisten them, let her hands fall to her sides.

"I am sorry," I said, as she started to rush to the far corner of the cave. "I am sorry," I repeated and she turned to listen. "You see, I don't want anyone to notice us. I want everyone to think that we are just on an errand for our parents."

Mario stood still while I took off his clothes. I knew where there was a forgotten pile of wood shavings, that the carpenter had not taken home with him to use as fuel for his wife's cooking; with a handful of these I began to scrub Mario. His eyes filled with tears and he sniveled.

"When we go, you must try not to cry or else everyone will notice us. You must follow your sister and me . . . and try not to cry."

The little one nodded his head and met my glance. His eyes were still moist but his expression was very serious. I smiled and he tried to smile back.

To dry himself, Mario sat down just outside the cave, on a rock. It was a stone that had fallen from the cliff during the last air-raid. Mario crossed his arms in front of him, each hand resting, palm up, on his thighs. 'He is so thin and weak,' I thought, 'that is why tears are his only response to everything.'

Anna was carrying the bucket to the corner of the cave. "Your ears and your neck," I called after her.

"I cannot get clean with dirty water," she replied.

"Bring me the bucket," I said, "but wash your feet in it first."

The wind came from the sea and smelled salty and fresh. When I arrived at the square — although it was only an hour after the sun had risen — there was already a long line of women. As I waited my turn, I looked about the piazza: here I had played and talked with the other children. Suddenly I became frightened of leaving Naples. I remembered how I had lost my cave and I grew angry. It was true that I had planned to go away from my cave because I had decided I ought to leave the city; but it had never occurred to me that it could be taken away from me. I had believed it to be my home; therefore, I had thought of giving it up; but if I could be ordered to leave from one day to the next, then it had never been mine.

Little Mario was still sitting near the entrance to the cave when I returned; still looking as earnest as before. Anna was standing inside in her dirty cotton petticoat. Her dress lay on the carpenter's bench. I could not tell what the material was; but it was brown and torn. I had never seen her wearing any other dress.

"At home . . . at your aunt's, didn't you have any other clothes?"

Anna shook her head and picked up the bucket.

"Finish washing; then dress the little one," I said. I walked to the mattress and sat down on it; I was so annoyed that I told myself that the carpenter had been right: I should have left alone.

Near my mattress I kept my shoes, my extra shirt, and an old pair of pants. Inside the mattress was a small cigarette box of metal; in this, I kept the ten *lire* which the count had given me; I had saved it to use when I left the city. I slid my hand in and took out the box, which I shoved into the one of my pockets that had no hole. My extra shirt I folded into a kerchief that I had found one day among the ruins. The old pair of pants I decided to leave behind, they were not worth carrying. I also owned a comb, though several of its teeth were missing, and a knife with a sharp point.

Anna and Mario were both dressed again. The little boy had a pair of worn shoes on, but Anna was barefooted. I wetted my hair and combed it. Mario's hair was still moist from having been washed. I tried to comb it, but there were many snarls, for it had not been combed in a very long time. Mario grimaced and tears appeared in his eyes, but he did not cry out. I gave the comb to Anna; when she was finished combing her hair she

apologized, for two more of the teeth were missing.
Once more I attempted to comb Mario's hair, and
this time I did manage to get it smooth.

"Come," I called.

I let Anna and Mario go out before me. The

thought that I had had about regretting that I was not going alone came back to me and filled me with disgust for myself.

It was now eight o'clock in the morning and at the piazza there were dozens of women and children waiting for water. Among them was a girl the same age as Anna. I knew her. Her name was Maria; but it was not the girl I was noticing as much as the dress she was wearing. It was not new, for although Maria had parents they were poor; yet compared to Anna's it seemed almost new.

I approached Maria boldly. "I want to buy your dress."

She was surprised; for though we would often sell things that we found and a boy had once sold his shirt for a bread, we seldom traded in our own clothes — maybe because none of us had any to spare. "I'll give you two *lire* for it," I continued.

"I'll think it over, while I wait to get the water," she replied.

She was almost at the end of the line. I was eager to get as far outside the city as possible that day. "It will take too long," I argued. "Come now, and we'll talk about it."

"I can't sell it anyway . . . My mother wouldn't let me. What do you want it for?"

"It is for her." I flung out my arm towards Anna, who was standing at the curb. "She has her only dress on." Anna must have guessed what I had said, for she looked embarrassed. "We are going away. Her aunt was killed. I am afraid we will be picked up."

Maria smiled pityingly towards Anna; and I said quickly, "Three *lire* and her dress!"

"I wouldn't want her dress. It is torn and dirty."

I looked at Maria. She was clean and her hair was combed.

"I have another dress at home," she said after a long pause. "You can buy that one for her. But I must get the water first."

"Is it as nice as the one you have on?" I asked, for now I wanted Anna to have that dress and no other.

"It is better than hers and clean."

I heard the contempt in her voice and I said, "You didn't wash your dress, your mother did . . . I will give you five *lire* for the dress you have on."

The girl shook her head and picked up her pitcher. There were still several women ahead of her.

I tried to convince myself that it could not matter so much, how we were dressed; but each time I glanced at Anna the argument seemed futile, for I wanted her to have a clean dress that was not torn.

"*Va bene* . . . All right," I said. "But hurry up," I added foolishly.

Time passed slowly as we watched the women fill their buckets and pitchers and carry them away on their heads. Before the war, a woman would always place a handkerchief or a clean rag on top of her head to protect her hair from what she carried; but now the cloth was usually missing. It was not only because even a small bit of material had value, but the women did not seem to care so much about their hair any more. Finally, it was Maria's turn, she filled up her pitcher and gestured for us to follow her.

The house that she lived in had not been damaged by any of the bombings. It was a better

house than most and the door looked almost new.

"Wait here for me," she said. "I will be right back. I don't want my mother to know."

"On which floor do you live?" I asked.

"The third," she replied and disappeared into the house.

We sat watching that building for so long that Anna suggested that Maria was playing a joke on us. I had just decided to go away, when we saw her coming out of the door. As she closed it behind her, we heard a woman's voice calling her name.

"Here it is," Maria held out the dress that she had carried crumpled in a bundle under her arm.

Although it was much better than the one Anna was wearing, the dress was well worn and was not nearly as pretty as the one Maria had on. It was a very plain dress and the belt was missing. "Two *lire*," I said.

"Three," the girl insisted and pretended that she was about to refold the dress.

I responded by shrugging my shoulders, to show my lack of interest in paying so much. "How do I know it even fits," I said nonchalantly. But then I saw Anna's face which had an expression that was a sad and curious mixture of defiance, shame, and desire. 'She wants the dress,' I thought. "You'll have to find a place for her to try it on," I said to Maria.

"Come," Maria ordered and led Anna into the house. Later Anna told me that she had been up in

Maria's home and that the mother was there; so Maria must have lied to us when she had said that her mother would not let her sell the dress.

When they returned to the street Anna was smiling broadly; the dress, if anything, was a little too big for her. Nervously, Anna's hands moved about her waist as she tried to adjust it better.

"All right," I agreed and gave Maria the three *lire*, which she slipped into her left shoe.

"Where are you going?"

The girl's question caught me by surprise. "North," I answered, but I might just as well have said south; or maybe not, for Naples was filled with people coming from the south where the misery was said to be greater than ours. Besides, the south was where my aunt and uncle lived; and there, too, was the churchyard where my mother was buried.

"To Cassino!" I blurted.

I knew that there was a city north of Naples by that name and that there was a monastery there.

11

"What is it like?"

I glanced at Anna questioningly. We were still in the outskirts of Naples and the sun had already set.

"The place we are going to, Cassino."

Along the street on which we were walking, the houses were low; each was surrounded by a high wall, behind which was a garden. Between many of the houses there were empty spaces.

"Cassino is a city," I replied without turning to look at her, for I did not want to admit that I did not even know whether it was a large or small city.

"I am tired." Little Mario was behind us. He looked very tired. His bare feet were covered with dust. I had taken his shoes away from him because I thought it was a waste for him to be wearing them now when it was so warm.

"Soon we will find a place to sleep," I said cheerfully, for I knew from experience that Mario would cringe at a frown, as if he had been promised a beating, while a smile could sometimes make him smile back. Already I was finding out the curse of being a leader: that though filled with doubt yourself, you can not allow it to show in your face or the tone of your voice. Ahead of us the road divided and there was a signpost. I was hoping that it would say, Cassino, and tell us how far away that city was.

One sign read: Aversa; the other: Caserta. In which direction was Cassino? The road to Caserta appeared less used, as if it would lead more quickly into the country. The name seemed familiar; maybe, one of the children we knew came from there. "We shall go via Caserta," I said to Anna. I almost laughed for I realized that the reason I had chosen this road was that the names sounded alike: Cassino, Caserta.

Soon we were in the country. There was pastureland. I was looking anxiously for a place for us to sleep for it was growing dark. It was warm and we could have slept anywhere in the fields; but I suspected that Mario would be frightened of lying out in the open without walls around the darkness. At last, in one of the fields I saw a small stone shed.

We would only have to climb over a low fence to get to it. There were vines growing in the fields so there would be no animals there.

I listened, half expecting a dog to bark as we approached the hut. In the cities dogs are afraid of human beings, even children; for city dogs are used to being kicked and having stones thrown at them; but the dogs of the country are different, they belong to the soil, to the farm, and will defend it against intruders.

No dogs barked. We entered the hovel, it had not been used for a long time. There was no door and part of the roof had fallen in. Some grape vines that had been cut off at the last pruning were stacked against a wall. I told Anna to select the thinner ones, while I cleared a corner of the hut for us to make our beds.

Even the finer of the vines were too hard to sleep upon, so Anna and I plucked some of the tall grass that grew around the hut to cover them. On top I spread out Anna's old dress and my shirt for Mario to sleep on.

"I'm hungry," Mario said. Before leaving the city I had bought a big bread; now I cut off three heavy slices of it. I gave the end piece which was the smallest to Mario because he was the youngest.

We had nothing to drink, nor could I recall having passed any wells near the vineyard; but not far beyond the hut was another field and separating it from this one was a row of trees. I could not see for it was too dark, but I knew that farmers often planted fruit trees at the edges of their property. Still eating my bread, I made my way to the trees. They were mostly fig — a fruit that is not ripe until August. Luckily, there was a single plum tree among them. The plums were small and hard and I did not pick very many, for unripe fruit could have given us stomach aches that would have made walking impossible.

"Here." I gave four plums each to Mario and Anna. They were sweeter than I had expected them to be; and I thought how fortunate the people in the country were, for here there was always fruit, even in the winter for that is the season of the oranges. Suddenly I felt proud. 'You have brought two children out of Naples, Guido,' I thought. 'You have fed them, and found a place for them to sleep. We shall be all right, Guido.'

I could hear little Mario and Anna sleeping, but I could not sleep myself. I was tired but I could not relax. My legs felt as though the blood were tickling them. I got up quietly and walked outside. There was almost a full moon and the stars were very pale in the sky. In the distance I heard the bark of a dog; such a sound makes one feel lonelier.

"Luna . . . Moon," I said the word out loud, but in a whisper for it is a magic word, as are the words you use in a prayer. "*Madre del Dio* . . . Mother of God," these are sacred words, but they are also magic ones and you say them slowly, softly. Even "bread" can be a magic word when you are hungry. Why are there magic words, words you only whisper? Why are they different from the words you shout in anger? A bat flew above my head, and I recalled that there had been many bats on my uncle's farm, but I had never seen one except at night when it is like a shadow flying above you. "Bat . . ." that was an ugly word, for most people do not like bats. *"Casa mia* . . . my house," that was soft and sweet. I smiled into the night, because I was having such strange thoughts; and I wondered if everyone had thoughts like that. Did grownups?

Would we be in Caserta tomorrow? What would that town be like? Like Messina? No, it must be smaller and it was not near the sea. Would it be a village like St. Marco, where I had walked with my mother? I reminded myself that St. Marco was in the mountains and so small that there was no roadsign pointing the way to it. As if moved by a gentle wind, my thoughts drifted to my mother, and I thought no more about the city of Caserta. In my mind I saw the stone fence on which my mother and I had sat. I remembered the lizards that I used to watch while she talked. Had I been strong . . . *duro* . . . as she had wished me to be? Had I been kind? I saw her face as it had been when she had been well; and I understood for the first time that although she had been very gentle, she, too, had been *duro* like iron.

I must have fallen asleep, for Anna's voice startled me. She was calling my name and she sounded frightened. I was sitting in the shadows of the grape vines, and she could not see me. "Anna," I called.

She was standing just outside the entrance to our hut and her face was filled with moonlight. "Guido," she whispered back. She said my name over and over again, as she came towards me. "Oh, Guido," she sank down on her knees beside me. "I thought you had gone! I thought you had gone!"

I stroked her hair; and for a long time we said nothing to each other. I was watching the clouds pass in front of the moon, when I heard her whisper, "I will remember to wash." Then she sat up. "You see, my aunt was sick for so long and we had only one room; they wouldn't let us use the kitchen. They wanted to throw us out. Now there is no house and they are all dead."

"It does not matter," I said and did not ask who *they* were. At that moment I felt that nothing that had happened to us in Naples mattered. But it was the moon and the soft night wind that gave me these thoughts; for everything that happens to you matters. Everything leaves a little scar: both the good and the bad; and when you grow up, then the scars are the story of your life.

"Come, we must sleep. We have far to go tomorrow."

I let Anna go in the hut and lie down before I entered. The moon shone through the doorway on Mario's face. He slept soundly and he was smiling.

Captured!

12

IT is not true that the poor always protect their own, nor that there is honor among thieves. There are those who are poor and yet steal from the poor as hungry rats will eat their own children.

We still were far from the city of Caserta when we first noticed the man following us. There were many people walking along the roads; sometimes we passed travelers and sometimes they passed us; but this man strode behind us at the same pace as ourselves. He was poor. On his head he wore a ragged soldier's cap; but he was barefooted and carried only a stick in his hands. I do not know why I did not like him, for he was not different from so many other wanderers whom we had seen: he did not look evil or even mean. Cain was stamped by a mark on his forehead, but this happened in the olden times, when God was nearer to man than He is today.

"Let us rest awhile," I suggested

A big tree threw its shadow across the road; underneath it the grass was green and near the trunk, there was a boulder. I sat down on the stone while Anna and the little one stretched out on the grass. Out of the corners of my eyes, I was watching the man who had been following us. He had halted when we had; and now he was taking a few steps towards us.

I heard a noise and I looked down the road. There was a farmer's cart coming. The stranger, too, had turned to see it.

"As soon as it gets here," I whispered to Anna, "we'll get up and walk beside the cart."

The peasant in the cart, the stranger, who had been following us, and we ourselves were the only ones on the road. As soon as the peasant was within earshot, I called to him, *"Buon' giorno* . . . Good morning."

He grunted by way of reply; yet we had only been walking behind him a few minutes when he said, "You can climb into the cart, if you want to."

"Grazia . . . thank you." I lifted Mario up by the elbows; but the sides of the cart were very high and I could not push him over them.

"Come let me." The stranger offered.

I didn't dare shout, 'Go way!' as I wanted to;

and the man took the boy from my hands and lifted him easily into the cart.

"Are they your children?" The peasant glanced at the stranger and I could see by his expression that he was thinking: 'Why should I tire out my horse with so many passengers?'

"Yes, we are going to Caserta; we have family there."

I could have shouted that this man was no relative of ours; but I knew that he would call me a liar and in an argument between grownups and children, a child's word is easily discounted.

"Well, you can get in for a while anyway." The owner of the cart smiled sourly and slid himself over a little, to make room on the board, which was his seat, for the stranger to sit down.

We children were in the bottom of the cart facing the rear. The backs of the men were behind and a little above us.

"What does he want?" Anna whispered to me.

I shook my head, for I did not know for certain what the stranger was planning. Little Mario was so pleased to be riding that he smiled alternately to his sister and me. I had heard of men who lived off the earnings of beggar children: taught them to steal and beat them if they refused to. Was the stranger that kind of man? I turned so that I could see his back. I noticed his hair, it was turning gray near his neck. He was no different from any other man. I slipped my hand into my pocket: my knife and the small metal box with six *lire* in it were still there.

"We could jump." It was Anna whispering to me again. I pointed to the boy. Mario could not jump; besides, either the farmer or the stranger would be sure to hear us and stop the cart. There would be two of them — for I believed that the peasant would help the stranger. No, it would be better to wait until we were alone with the man.

"What does it matter that you get good prices," the peasant was saying, "when the money is worth nothing?" He wiped his forehead with his hand and said sadly, "Ah, that war!" Then he shook his head.

"You have food, at least. In Naples, more than half the people go to sleep with an empty stomach."

"Yes, food we have, thanks to God. But for how long . . . for how long? The soldiers steal and the other ones — " The farmer stopped speaking. He realized that we probably belonged to the "other ones," the homeless ones, who had left Naples and the other cities of the south, driven to the roads by hunger and the hope that somewhere, further north, there would be food and work.

"Some of them are bad," the stranger remarked, implying that he was not one of them. But in the next breath, he spoke threateningly, "I have seen them knife an old man for a bread."

"*Dio mio* . . . My God! Why didn't they just take the bread? Why did they have to knife him?"

The farmer turned to look back at us, as if the sight of children could reassure him that everything was all right.

"They were bad ones." The stranger laughed; but his laughter was ugly.

The farmer was silent. He shook the reins making the horse walk faster. At the first crossroad, he pulled the horse to a halt. With a tremble in his voice, he said, "I turn here. The road to Caserta is straight ahead."

"Thank you, Grandpa," the stranger muttered, but he did not get up.

I lifted Mario over the side of the cart and dropped him onto the road; then I jumped down myself.

"Could you help some unfortunates?" The voice was not that of a beggar.

The peasant looked desperately up and down the roads: there was no one to be seen, nor could we hear any vehicle coming.

"They are motherless and we are starving." Again his words did not carry as much meaning as his tone, which said: 'Give me your money or I will take your life.'

"Mother of God!" the peasant exclaimed and I followed the direction of his gaze. The stranger's hands were resting on his knees; in one of them there was a knife. It was a long thin knife; the kind that is better for killing a man than cutting bread.

Slowly the peasant took out his purse. It was

made of leather and well worn. His hands trembled so much that he could not untie the strings, and he let the unopened purse fall into the thief's lap. The moment the thief had the purse in his left hand, the knife disappeared from his right. It all happened so quickly that one almost doubted that the knife had ever been there at all.

"*Buon' passeggiata* . . . Have a nice trip." The stranger was standing beside the cart and grinning insolently at the peasant, whose face was now red from rage.

Using the ends of the reins, the farmer began to beat the rump of the horse savagely, as if by striking the poor beast, he were hitting the thief. The horse jumped in his shaft and pulled the cart forward, making the peasant almost tumble out of his seat. Yet as soon as he gained his balance, he beat the horse again and the animal broke into a gallop down the side road.

"Remember that money is worth nothing!" the stranger shouted after him and laughed. Now he turned to us. "Well, my children, tell your father your names."

Anna held little Mario behind her and said nothing. I looked up into the man's face.

"If you listen to me, I shall be a good father. If you don't . . ." The man made a wide swing with his arm to indicate what he would do, if we didn't obey him.

"You are nothing to us. Go away," I said. I wanted to call him a thief, to call him every hateful word I knew, yet I said no more.

"You stay with me and you will eat." The man shook the peasant's purse at us. "If you try to run away, I will catch you and make you wish that you were dead." His voice caressed the word "dead"; and he grinned at Anna long after he had finished speaking.

Anna's eyes were terror filled and the little one was puckering up his face, getting ready to cry. I was not as frightened as they were, for the very violence of his threats showed how weak he was. What would he do if we escaped? How, among the mass of refugees walking the roads of Italy, would he find us again? No, once we were gone, he would look for some other children who would fit his devices, some other homeless orphans whom he could beat into stealing or begging for him.

"We will follow you." I said the words lightly; then I turned my face, so that he could not see my features, and I winked at Anna.

The Thief

13

"By Our Lady, that fat farmer was frightened. His stomach was tight with fear." The thief laughed.

As if I, too, found the peasant's fright for his life amusing, I grinned; for I had decided that it would be far easier for us to make our escape, if I first could persuade our self-made father to trust us.

"There are two kinds of people in the world: those who steal and those who are stolen from; the fishes in the sea and the fishermen who catch and eat them." The man laughed again.

'The thief is a braggart who is fond of hearing himself talk,' I thought. But what he said lingered in my mind, for somewhere I had heard those words before . . . The German officer on the day that I had met Anna and Mario! He, too, had talked

about fishes and compared human beings to them.
He, too, had thought of himself as a fisherman, or
at least as one of the big fish who ate the little ones.
'They are strong men,' I thought, 'but they have no
kindness and they wear themselves out, without
ever having enjoyed the beauty of the strength,
which is to protect the weak not to threaten them.

Ahead of us on the left, a road branched off. It
led to a small village, we could see the church. The
thief stood still for a moment. Mario was so tired
that he sat down in the dust beside the road. The
man glanced at the child and then with a cast of his
head motioned for us to follow him down the nar-
rower road.

"Let us run now," Anna whispered; but I took
Mario's hand and started to follow the thief.

"We have no bread to sell." The woman in the
little bar next to the church frowned and looked
away; but the stranger sat down at one of the two
tables and put his elbows on the rough wood of the
table-top. "Bring us some food. I will pay."

The woman was staring at us children and I
smiled towards her. "Are they your children?"
she asked in a tone of doubt, which made me hope
that in her we might find a friend: someone who
would believe us.

The thief sighed and shoved one of his hands
through his hair. "Their mother died. I am taking
them north to my sister."

The woman smiled at Mario and then at the thief. So easily, had she been convinced. 'Grownups will always believe each other,' I thought bitterly.

"We have some beans," she said, "but it will cost two *lire* to give portions to all of you."

The thief threw up his arms. "Mother of God. How everyone lives off the poor, the homeless. It is a wonder that any man or woman in Italy can say his prayers before he sleeps, knowing that little children are out at night, hungry and cold."

The woman looked away and the thief pointed at little Mario. "We have walked all day; and the little one is so tired that he is almost asleep on his feet. His mother would cry in heaven, if she could see him. But I will pay. We are not beggars — not yet, at least. But give me a bottle of wine, for I am thirsty."

Furtively the woman glanced over her shoulder towards the door that led to the kitchen, and beyond which was probably the bedroom; then she whispered, "I dare not give it to you free for my husband is very hard with beggars; but give me one *lira*, and you shall have the food and the wine, too. I have some money that I was going to buy a candle with for Our Lady. I will give it to him and he will never know."

"May Our Lady bless you, kind Signora," the thief said and drew a *lira* from his pocket but he did not show the stolen purse.

"For the sake of the little ones."

'She has no children,' I thought, 'And she longs for one. She is lonely without a child.' For she spoke to us so softly, so timidly, as a woman who has never had a child of her own often does. When she saw that Anna and I were still standing, she said almost apologetically, "Sit down, children."

"Grazia . . . Thank you," Anna and I replied both at once.

"What is worse: hunger or thirst?" We were through eating and the thief poured the last of the wine from the bottle into his glass, as he spoke.

"They say that the man about to be hung envies the one who is to be shot . . . But who knows." I was repeating something that I had once heard the carpenter say in an argument with old "sack of bones"; but my answer pleased the thief.

"Tomorrow, we shall be in Caserta. It was once a rich town. The King of Naples used to live there in the summer. Where there once was enough for a Bourbon, there should be a little bit left for us."

I agreed, but silently I was saying to myself, 'Tomorrow we shall not be with you.'

As if the thief had guessed my thoughts, he bent forward and stretched himself across the table. "While you beg," he whispered, "I will keep the little one with me; and if you don't bring back what you get, then I will beat you until you do."

I was looking at Anna. I could not guess whether she was angry or frightened; but when I happened to glance into her lap, I saw both of her hands clenched into fists. Little Mario was asleep in his chair and heard nothing.

"If you give us something to eat, we shall beg for you. But if you beat and starve us, we will run away and then you can keep the little one."

The thief was silent for a moment. His brow was wrinkled. I realized that he was a fool who planned nothing. His theft of the farmer's purse was something he had thought of on the spur of the moment; and probably the idea of having children beg for him had not occurred to him until he found himself following us. This would make our escape easier; though it was also a warning that he was dangerous. Men like the thief commit murder for ten *lire;* they are brutes whose appetites and passions think for them.

"If you run away, I will kill him." He flung out his hand towards the sleeping head of Mario. The little child in his exhaustion had let his head rest, face down, on the table.

"Why should we run away? If you take care of us, we will have no reason to run away. It is good for children to have a grownup to protect them."

The thief's lips turned upwards in what he probably thought was a kindly smile. "I will be good to you," he said.

The thief arranged for us to sleep in the stable behind the bar. It was long since it had been used, but one could still smell that a horse had once been kept there. I liked the smell, it reminded me of my cave; and I wished that I was back there, until I remembered how easily it had been taken away from me. I tried not to think of the cave any more.

It was a small stable. There were no windows and only one door, which opened inward. The thief propped a broken beam up against it, as he said jokingly, "We wouldn't want any thieves to get in." Then lying down in front of the door, so that anyone who wanted to leave would have to step over him, he added, "Nor any little thief to run away, either."

I was carrying Mario, who was still asleep in my arms. I laid him down as far away from the door as possible, and Anna stretched herself out next to him. Loudly I said, "Go to sleep. We shall have far to walk tomorrow."

I sat down with my back against the wall and whispered to Anna, "Later . . . later." Knowing that she would want to say something, I reached out my hand to find her face in the darkness, to warn her to keep still.

I did not want either Anna or Mario to sleep; but within seconds Anna's regular breathing indicated that she, too, was deeply asleep. When the thief began to snore, I crawled towards him on all fours.

A shaft of light from the moon came in through the space between the wall and the poorly hinged door. It shone on the man's sleeping face.

He looked peaceful, as if he had never had an evil thought or done an evil deed. What had made him what he was? While we had been eating, I had thought to myself, 'I shall kill the man if need be.' And my hand had reached into my pocket, where I kept my knife. But now, I realized that I could not do it while he slept, and when he was awake it was impossible for he was much stronger than I. I noticed one of his hands; it was resting against the door, but it was knotted tightly as if he were ready to strike out. Some time, long ago, he had been a child my age; and before that a little one like Mario. 'What happens to children when they grow up?' I asked myself but I found no answer.

The roof of the stable was low. In the corner where we were lying, it was only a few inches above my head. I raised up both my hands. The roof was made of tiles! I smiled into the darkness and rubbed my hands together. Very carefully I removed one tile and then another. The moon shone down upon Anna's face and she turned in her sleep. Silently, I kneeled down beside her and whispered in her ear, "Anna, wake up!"

When she finally opened her eyes, her expression was one of bewilderment, for she did not know where she was. I placed my finger in front of my mouth to tell her not to speak; then I pointed to the hole in the roof. I did not need to explain to her what to do; she smiled and began to help me at once.

When we had removed the sixth tile, the hole was big enough for us to climb through. Grabbing the freed edge of the wall, I pulled myself up, so that I could look out. Beyond the wall was a small garden and beyond that, the road. 'If only there are no dogs,' I thought.

Anna was trying to wake her little brother. The child was sleeping so soundly that even though she shook him roughly, he slept on. At last she yanked him into a sitting position; but his little head dropped onto his chest without his eyes opening. Anna looked angrily at the boy and was about to pull his hair, but I pushed her arm away. I stroked Mario's forehead; he squinted and then looked at me beseechingly.

I turned his head upwards towards the hole. He nodded to show that he understood. Anna climbed through the opening, and jumped the short distance to the ground. I lifted Mario. One of his feet kicked my face accidentally, and I almost cried out. I managed to get him up onto the wall, but he was facing the wrong way. I tried to make him understand that he must turn around; but he was so frightened that he kept on shaking his head, while he clutched the rafters with all his strength. Finally, I took hold of his legs and pushed them up to the top of the wall, forcing him to face in the oppo-

site direction. I heard Anna whispering to him to jump, but he was terrified. All the while I kept glancing back at the thief. Suddenly he moved his arm, the one that had rested against the door. I pushed little Mario off the wall. He fell on top of his sister and cried out her name. As quickly as I could I climbed over the wall and let myself drop to the other side.

Anna was waiting for me, holding her hand across Mario's mouth. The moon shone brightly. "Run to that tree," I whispered and pointed to an olive tree at the end of the garden; the leaves were silver with moonlight. Anna picked up her brother in her arms and carried him.

I stood still for a moment beneath the opening in the roof, listening. All was silent inside the stable. It was a good wine that the thief had drunk.

"In which direction should we go, Guido?" Anna asked when we reached the road beyond the village. Although the stable with the sleeping thief was now far behind us, she spoke in a whisper.

"Not to Caserta," I responded and to my surprise, I, too, spoke in a hushed voice. 'It is night,' I thought. 'It is the darkness that makes us whisper.'

I looked in both directions; not far ahead there was a road leading to the right, and opposite it there was a road sign. "That way," I said; and when we reached the sign I declared, "We are going to Capua."

"Is that on the way to Cassino?"

I smiled: What was Cassino but a word like Caserta, yet Anna wanted that town to be more than a name, so I said out loud, "Yes, Capua is on the way to Cassino and it is a good town."

14

We did not stop at Capua; the town was filled with soldiers. I bought a bread from one of them. I did not beg for we had eaten a good meal the night before and I still had five *lire*. There are those who will beg even when their stomachs are filled; but they are not many. To most people it is as difficult to stretch out their right hands, palms upturned, as it is to steal. Perhaps even more so, for I have heard of cities in the world where there are no beggars, but never of one — not even in America — which had no thieves.

It was nearing noon. The sun was burning on our backs. I watched the side of the road for shade and a place where we might rest. We reached a fork, but there were no roadsigns. One road was less traveled than the other; because of our meeting with the thief, I decided to take it.

"Are you sure you took the right one?" Anna asked timidly.

Oddly enough, my smile which was caused by inability to answer — for how could I know which was the right road? — seemed to reassure her.

"The little one is very tired," she whispered.

Mario was so weary that he walked with his head bent; and I was sure that his eyes saw nothing, not even the dirt beneath his feet. Fortunately, there were some large trees growing in a field not far ahead.

In the shadows of the trees it was quite cool. A brook ran nearby. We drank from it and ate most of the bread that we had bought in Capua. The boy fell asleep before he had eaten the last of his bread. The crust dropped out of his hand when sleep relaxed him. I picked it up, so I would be able to give it to him when the time came to wake him.

"That man . . ."

I nodded, for I knew it was the thief whom Anna

wanted to talk about. "What would he have done
with us?"

I shrugged my shoulders. Anna was lying down
beside her sleeping brother. I was sitting near her.

"He made me afraid, not because he might beat
me, it wasn't that." And with a burst of pride she
said, "I am not afraid of a beating." She was silent
for a while, then she touched my hand and whispered, "Guido, sometimes the grownups act as if
they had a secret, some shameful secret. And then
I am afraid of them. He was like that, like a beast
in the night, that you have dreamed about, who in
the daytime, you think must have been a lion, but
in the night, it is just a beast and you have no name
for it." Anna looked away from me and let her
glance rest on her brother. "Mario is only afraid of
being hit; and if he dreams of an animal it is always
one that will eat him up. . . . He is a child."

And for the first time, in the tone of her voice,
when she said "child," I realized that Anna loved
her brother.

"We are children, too," I insisted. "Grownups
may be different than we are; but that fellow was
just a thief."

Anna spoke very slowly for she was tired. "Yes,
he was a beast, but sometimes, Guido, I think I see
that secret in the faces of men who are not: men
who are kind and they look sad because of it, but
they also look frightening." When she stopped
talking her eyes were half-closed.

"We shall never see him again. Don't worry about him." I thought of old "sack of bones," and his belief that only the devil lives.

Anna was falling asleep for it took her a long time to reply. "You are a boy, Guido . . . And boys are sometimes very silly."

I wanted to protest, but she was asleep. I wondered whether boys were more silly than girls. I had always thought that girls were the sillier: didn't they giggle the most? I didn't want to sleep; still I lay down for I was very tired. "The beast," I whispered and remembered a big tomcat with one eye that had lived near my cave. Anna's words came to me separately: "Secret . . . Beast . . . Men . . ."

It was a fly sitting on my nose that woke me up. It walked from the tip of my nose to the bridge and then down to the tip again. I shook my head and it flew to my forehead; then it leaped to my lips. At last, I sat up. The sun was already low in the horizon and the shadows of the trees were long and dark. Anna and Mario were still asleep. The little one's head was lying on his sister's arm.

The landscape was so peaceful. As I kneeled down to drink of the water of the brook, I heard its song; and I waited not wanting to disturb it. When I had drunk, I washed my face and in the early evening air, it felt almost cold. Far in the distance was a shepherd with his flock. 'This is the way it always has been,' I thought. 'There have been shepherds and brooks and tall green grass and great trees.' And suddenly I was happy. I picked a blade of grass and chewed the soft end of it. 'Tomorrow . . . Yesterday . . . And even when I am dead, it will be like this. And there have been others like me and there will be more of us.' My thoughts surprised me for I had never had thoughts like that before: thoughts that could make me love everything about me, everything I saw.

"Wake up," I whispered. Anna did not respond and I shook her gently. Slowly she opened her eyes; then she asked softly, "Did I fall asleep?"

I laughed and Anna laughed too as she sat up. The little one, his sleep having been disturbed by Anna's movements, rolled over on his tummy and hid his head in his arms. We watched him. He was like a little puppy. I leaned across Anna and patted his head.

"How far is it to Cassino?"

I shrugged my shoulders, I was annoyed. How should I know and did it matter? Wasn't one place as good as another? We had only left the brook a short while before. I had given Mario his morsel of bread and we had all drunk from the brook; yet already we were tired.

"What if Cassino is not a good city? What if it is full of soldiers as Capua was, and there is no bread?" I had tried to ask the question lightly, so I could say that I was merely joking, if my suggestions upset Anna.

"Then we'll go somewhere else," she said.

"But all the time, you keep asking about it."

"I like the idea of there being a place beyond this." She looked towards the horizon. "It seems less empty. Everything has to have a name, like my name is Anna and yours is Guido. And a dog is called a dog and a cat, a cat. I like to think we are going towards some place. And when it has a name, you know it exists, and you can see it in front of you."

I was relieved and yet without knowing why, I was more annoyed than before. "How do you know what it looks like?"

"I have an aunt, my father's sister, who lives in New York. If Cassino is no good, we can go to New York."

I laughed for I knew that New York was across a great sea in a country called America, and that one could not walk to it. "And do you know what New York looks like because you know the name?"

Anna was silent for several minutes. "It is a very rich city," she suddenly began. "Not like Naples. But there is water like there is around our city, and it has little islands like Ischia and Capri. It has many churches with great big spires; and every one is of gold; and when the sun comes up in the morning, they look like golden sewing needles. Around the city is a great wall, that goes down to the sea.

And the sea is filled with colored fishes. Inside the
city there are palaces and gardens and children
who play in swings, like the ones on a chocolate
box. And everyone is happy."

Once, while I was still living with my mother in
Messina, I had seen a postcard from New York.
It had been of a great bridge; there were no palaces
or churches to be seen on it. "How do you know
that New York is like that?"

Anna shook her head confidently. "Is America
not a rich country? Does not everyone who goes
there to live return to Italy a *signore*, no matter how
poor he was when he left?"

This, I had to admit, was true. In Sicily, I had
heard of many poor people who had spent only a
few years in America and had come back to the
villages where they were born to buy houses and
live well. "But maybe they don't build churches,"
I said hesitantly.

Anna smiled and said firmly, "Is not Rome richer
than Naples? Do they not have finer churches than
we, and palaces and parks? Well, Rome is poorer
than Naples if you compare it to New York; and
therefore, they must have even finer churches and
even greater palaces. Don't the rich want everything to be beautiful? Don't even poor women like
pretty dresses? Sometimes they like them even
more than food."

I laughed and agreed with Anna. I remembered
that my mother had been proud of her best dress,

for though she always had had to wear black after my father died, this dress had been of a shiny material and there had been lace around the neck.

It was dark now, but the night was warm, and soon the moon would be up. The stars had already appeared in the sky. The carpenter had once told me that they were suns, as our sun that rises in the morning. I marveled at how far away they must be. I wondered whether each of them had its own earth, and whether each earth had children living on it. Would there be a boy named Guido on one of them, and would he be poor like me? And would there be sweet summer winds and dusty roads just as there were here? Or would it be like New York? Were there palaces in which everything was made of gold? Would there be no poor people at all? And no war? And no soldiers?

Beyond a hill, I saw the light of the moon. Slowly, as if someone were pulling it up on a string, ever so gently, it rose. The leaves of the olive tree reflected the light; and on the other side of the road the evenly spaced rows of vines appeared as if they had been drawn by a pencil.

"Let us sleep here for tonight," I said, "in the vineyard. No one will see us there."

I lifted Mario over the ditch and into the field. When I put him down, he would not let go of my hand. 'He is afraid of the moon,' I thought. I squeezed his hand gently; after all, he was only four years old.

The Bridge

15

"We are going towards the sea. Is Cassino by the sea?"

We were out of the hills and the land stretched flat in front of us; and as Anna had remarked, we were nearing the sea. I had slept badly in the vineyard and I was very tired. A little way back, the signpost had been the choice of Sessa Aurunca or Formia. I had taken the road to Formia. Now I was sorry, for Formia must be very far away, there was no view of anything but meadow and farmland, in spite of our being able to see a great distance.

At the edge of the road there was a gate and a path led to a house far back, beyond the fields. On the other side of the gate a little dirt road led into a hollow, shaded by a very large tree. We had stolen some tomatoes, which I had carried in my shirt, for it was too hot to wear it. I gave two tomatoes each to Anna and Mario, and we sat down on a stone next to the gate to eat them. When I had finished eating, my fingers aimlessly made marks in the dust that covered the flat stone. It was marble and there were letters chiseled into it. I made Anna and Mario get up and we cleared the stone of the dirt and dust that lay upon its surface. I recognized the many letters, but I could not read the words, and I guessed that they must be in Latin like the words the priests speak.

We heard a great rumbling and I ran out into the road. Coming towards us from the north, in that direction where Formia must be, was a long column of trucks. They were led by a tank and there was a great clatter as its iron tracks pressed against the asphalt of the road.

"Let's go!" I called to Anna and Mario. We ran down the narrow dirt road next to the gate.

The trucks were filled with soldiers; and there were cars on which cannons were mounted. "They are Germans," I whispered to Anna; though there was no need to speak softly for the noise of the vehicles was so loud that no one could have heard us from the road, even if I had shouted.

"I wonder where they are going?" Anna asked.

"Maybe to Naples," I replied.

I was thinking of my father. Had he driven a tank like the one we had just seen? I tried to remember what his uniform had looked like, from that single memory I had of sitting on his lap; but I couldn't. He was dead! That was the only thing I knew about him. I did not know how he had died, nor do I think that my mother had, for she never spoke of it. The last car was passing. It was a small open car and there were three officers in it. Slowly the noise of the motors faded and the dust in the air settled once more on the ground. 'How many,' I asked myself, 'how many of these soldiers would die?'

I glanced up at the great tree that grew on the embankment high above us. It was the tallest tree I had ever seen. The dirt road continued to cut deeper and deeper into the earth, because of the tall tree's shade, it appeared almost like a tunnel. 'It is a magic road,' I thought, 'like a road that you walk in your dreams.'

Anna must have had the same thought, for she started walking by herself down the road. Little Mario ran after her and grabbed her hand. I think he felt the magic, too, but it may have frightened him. "Anna!" I called. She turned her head and smiled but she did not stop.

Soon we could see the house that had its gate out on the highway. A path led through a smaller gate down to the road on which we were walking. "A real *signore* lives there, not just a farmer," Anna remarked. We heard a woman shouting at someone in the house, but we could not see her.

Beyond the house, the embankment fell away and the earth again became level with the road, but only for a short distance; then it sloped down into a valley with green grass and trees. The road, however, continued above the valley; on either side of it grasses, bushes, and even small trees grew.

"It is a magic road," I said aloud.

Where the land began to descend into a valley, the path was paved with large stones; stones that were worn smooth like the statues on the great cathedral in Naples. Both Anna and I hesitated; we were frightened to step on a road whose sides were covered with grasses, a road which hung in the air. Still our feet told us that it was solid enough and we walked onward. Each of us had hold of one of Mario's hands.

When we reached what seemed to be the middle of it, I tried to look over the sides. I caught sight of a stream and trees; but I did not dare to go too close to the edge. Anna, too, was looking down; and then suddenly both of us started to run the rest of the way across.

I heard someone crying behind me, and I went back for Mario. Once on the other side of the valley, we looked back, half-expecting the road to have disappeared behind us. It hadn't. I could see the big house on the other side of the gorge.

The "magic" road we had been walking on was a bridge. But it was unlike any bridge I had ever seen before. It was made of red bricks and had great arches. It reminded me of a wrecked ship

I had seen on a beach in Sicily. It had stood on the sand — half broken by the wind and sea and somehow, though it had been abandoned, it had looked more like a ship than many of the ones I had seen in the port.

"It must be old," Anna said.

"I think it is from ancient times, like Pompey."

At the side of the bridge there was a little path which led down into the dale, and we decided to follow it. I could hear water running and once between two boulders, I caught sight of water. 'It is still a magic place,' I thought and shivered a little. The stream which flowed in the depth of the valley was about four yards wide and about a foot deep. At the edge of it was a house and from that there came a great rumbling sound.

"Good morning," a man greeted us from the door of the house.

"*Buon' giorno, Signore,*" I answered back as politely as I could, for he had smiled at us and I guessed him to be a kind man. The wrinkles in his face spelled more laughter than anger. "We are travelers, Signore."

The man smiled again, as if he found nothing extraordinary in three children traveling alone. "And where are you from?"

At first, I thought of answering Messina, but I knew that people in the north were not fond of Sicilians; they think us thieves and bandits. Neapolitans are also mistrusted, so I said, "We are from St.

Marco in Calabria." Because I knew he could not have heard of it, I added, "It is a very small village, Signore."

From behind the door to the house, I could hear a constant drone. I took a step sideways, so that I could see inside.

"It is a watermill," the man said.

"A watermill!" I exclaimed. "How can you use water for a mill?"

"Come in and I will show you."

Little Mario came no nearer than the threshold, but Anna and I entered the house. The room was filled with dust from flour. A big stone was turning around on top of another stone. Wheels and shafts were moving, and they groaned and shrieked as if their movements were painful to them.

"It's the water beneath that makes everything work. It is an underground stream, that comes from high up in the mountains."

I recalled the place where I had seen the water rushing far below me, between the boulders, when we descended into the valley.

The miller pulled three levers, and the machinery stopped. Now the underground waters flowed uninterrupted into a little river.

As there was no more noise to terrify him, Mario joined us. He walked up to the miller and took his hand. It was a strange thing for him to do for he was usually very frightened of strangers.

"I'm hungry," the little one said.

The man's face darkened, as if he were going to be angry. Quickly, I grabbed Mario's free hand and tried to pull him away; but the miller only grinned at the boy and tousled his hair. "I shall see what I can find for you, but I wasn't expecting guests." Turning to me, he asked, "Is he your brother?"

"Yes," I replied. "And this is my sister, Anna." I had said it without hesitation, but now I glanced at Anna; she did not seem to have noticed. At that moment it struck me that I knew nothing about Anna. Although I had told my story to her; she had never mentioned her father or her mother to me. I did not even know whether she was an orphan, or whether somewhere she and Mario had parents who were still alive.

The miller shared out his lunch among us. "Here," he said and passed his bottle to me. The wine was sour as peasant wine usually is, but it was heavy and strong.

"We slept outside all night in a vineyard," Mario complained to the miller and gesturing towards us he added bitterly, "And they always give me the smallest piece of bread."

The miller laughed. "No one lives in the mill," he began hesitantly; but as he spoke he grew more enthusiastic about his suggestions. "I live in Sessa, a couple of miles from here. Now if some travelers came along, and they were honest and they wanted a place to stay for a while; I might want them to watch the mill for me at night, there might be thieves about with so many people on the road." The miller put his arm around Mario's shoulder. "Now up the valley a little way there lives a farmer. I know him well. He keeps an eye on the mill when I am not here. I am sure he would like someone to help him in the fields. He won't give you any money; but then today I think food is worth more than money."

The miller paused and Anna said quickly, "We would like to stay." The miller with some ceremony shook hands with Anna and me; but little Mario he picked up and kissed.

Before the miller left for his house in Sessa, he showed us the small storeroom that was next to the mill, although it could not be entered from it. "You can sleep here," he explained. From the mill he brought us some sacks. "They are dusty. You will have to shake them out, but they are good to sleep on."

He threw the sacks on the floor of the empty room. "I am locking up the mill, but if you see any strangers around, you just call the farmer."

I was about to protest that I wouldn't know who was a stranger and who wasn't, when I noticed the miller's broad grin: he was not worrying about thieves. With a large key he locked the mill door; then he said good-bye and that he would see us the next morning. We watched him climb the path beside the bridge. He was middle-aged. He walked a little stooped, as if he were carrying a sack of flour across his shoulders.

"Whom are you beating?"

Anna let her hand fall to her side. "The sack, naturally."

Her face was still angry and flushed, and I laughed. "I'll bet it was the thief you were beating."

Anna laughed, too.

"The miller is a good man," I said because Anna had grown silent again and was bringing her switch with increasing force down upon the sacks which we were trying to rid of flour and dust.

"Why do the other ones have to exist? Why does God let them live? Why doesn't Our Lady mark them so that everyone will know what they are like and stone them to the end of the world?!" Anna threw away her stick. She sat down on the grass and to my surprise, she began to cry.

"Don't!" I exclaimed, for as soon as little Mario heard his sister sob, he, too, began to cry. "Maybe, Our Lady does; but we just can't read the mark?" I kneeled down beside the girl and stroked her hair.

Anna pushed my hand away. "My father is like that man. He cares for no one but himself! He laughs at everyone."

I looked away. "Where is your father now?"

"In prison," Anna answered and dried her tears

with the back of her hand. "In prison," she repeated, "and I hope he dies there."

The hatred in her voice frightened me. The sun was setting; and the valley was half in shadow and half clothed in gold. "There are good men and bad men; and maybe, God made it that way."

Anna echoed, "Maybe." Then she laughed, pushed her little brother over in the grass and started tickling him.

16

THE SUMMER passed into fall. We worked at the farm in the valley. We ate. We played in the stream. We were happy. I know I ought to be able to tell you about it, yet I cannot, for while a nightmare will stay with you like hunger, when you awake from a happy dream, you have no memory of it. We took stones of the stream and built a pool that was waist-deep to play in. We picked flowers, caught frogs, and played *boccia* with stones. The days flowed like the waters beneath the mill; and I think it was the memory of that summer which made it possible for us to bear the winter that was to come.

In the valley, we only heard of the war. From the miller and the farmer, we knew what was happening. To me the war seemed to be something that existed, like a storm or an earthquake. Yet I could not agree with the farmer who said it was God's will. I spent much time thinking about it, and I tried to speak to Anna of my thoughts, but she did not understand me. The war frightened her: it was bad, it was evil; therefore, she would not talk about it.

It was on the day that Italy surrendered that the Germans came. The miller had brought the news of the armistice; and both he and the farmer rejoiced. They were drinking *grappa* and toasting the peace. We were all talking about the Americans. To us, Italians, America is not a foreign country, though it is beyond a tremendous ocean, it is the place where your uncle, your brother, or your children have gone. It is a land of wealth, and in a way, it is our country, too; for we speak of it as if it were less different and much closer than France or Germany.

"To peace!" the miller held up his glass.

We were sitting under the grape vines, the grapes above us were heavy, ripe for picking.

"To peace!" the farmer answered. But he had no sooner brought his glass to his lips, than his expression became confused — he was listening to something.

Soon we all heard the noise of the motors coming nearer and nearer. The sound came from the road to Sessa; but that road was so bad that cars never drove down it. The miller and the farmer got up from the table, and we all ran up the little hill behind the farmer's house to get a better view.

A large truck with a gun, on two rubber tires, trailing behind it, had halted near the approach to the bridge.

"But the war is over," the miller said, while we watched the soldiers jump out of the back of the truck.

"They are Germans," the farmer said and pointed to the officer, who stood in front of the truck, with one of his hands leaning on the headlight. He was looking at the bridge.

The gun was an anti-aircraft cannon. The Germans cleared a bit of ground in the vineyard, above the bridge, and installed themselves there. There were eight of them: one officer, a sergeant, and six ordinary soldiers. They came to the farm for water and to buy vegetables; and they bathed in the little pool in the stream below the bridge. They were polite, especially the officer, who spoke Italian well. He was very young and made every effort to be friendly. He played with Mario and the boy ran to him whenever he saw him. In the beginning Anna and I kept away from the Germans, yet we saw them every day, and this created a feeling that we knew each other, even though we seldom spoke. What finally made us become friends was a coin.

I was sitting under the bridge thoughtlessly letting the pebbles and the sand sift through my fingers, when I noticed a little green stone. When I picked it up, to look at it more closely, I recognized that it was not a stone, but a piece of metal, all green with tarnish. Rubbing it, I could see that there was something impressed on it, a design and around it letters, but I could not read them.

I was on my way up to the farm to show it to the peasant, when I met the young German officer; and I told him of my discovery instead. Perhaps it was because he had given some sugar to little Mario the day before.

"It is a coin!" The young officer squinted his eyes; then in a tone of wonder, he added, "A Roman one!"

"A Roman one?" Puzzled, I echoed his words. Did not the people of Rome use the same coins as we did in Naples? And this little piece of metal, green with tarnish, how did he know that it was a coin?

"It is from ancient times," he explained.

"From the days of Pompey," I said, glad that I had not told him what I had been thinking.

The German laughed and turned the coin over and over again in the hollow of his hand. It seemed to me that as he scrutinized it, his face changed; that it became milder and dreamlike.

'It is a magic coin,' I thought.

"It is from the time of Vespasian." The German officer had brought the coin, which he had cleaned, so that the letters could be read, with him down to the mill. It now had the color of copper; there were only a few specks of green to be seen. "I let it soak in vinegar overnight," he explained.

Again I was surprised by the excitement in the man's voice. Why did this coin mean so much to a man who commanded a cannon and eight other men? "Who was Vespasian?" I asked.

"An Emperor of Rome, who reigned . . ." The German knitted his brow, trying to recall the dates. "About sixty years after the birth of Christ." Looking away from me, he scowled. "I used to know the dates of all the emperors."

I didn't want to give up the coin because I thought that it might bring me luck; but I knew the German wanted it and I decided it would be wiser to give it to him. "You may have it," I said.

The German laughed; then when I glanced up at him, he said seriously, "No, it is yours."

He held the coin out to me and I shook my head. 'If I had not offered it to him, he wouldn't have thought of giving it back to me,' I said silently to myself. Perhaps this is not true; perhaps his laughter only meant that he did not have to give it back to me because he was a German officer. The miller had told us of other German soldiers who had come to his house in Sessa and demanded sacks of flour; and we had heard that there were farms where the oil and wine were taken away by the Germans.

The German told me to come closer and he held the coin up to the sunlight. "That is the symbol of the emperor."

The design reminded me of a key and I said so. "No," the officer said. "It is the staff, like a sceptre." With his finger he covered the face of the coin that was now in the palm of his hand.

"Was he a good emperor?" I asked, as the German carefully put the coin in his breast pocket.

Gazing at the old bridge, he answered me. "He was not as great as some of the others were. Still, he was a strong man."

"A strong man?" For the first time I understood that the meaning of words can depend upon who is saying them. "Like Mussolini?"

The officer laughed scornfully. "Not like Mussolini, any more than Italians are like Romans."

Suddenly the officer's face seemed ugly to me. "Good!" I said. "I am glad!" For at that moment, it seemed to me right that the Italians should not be Romans.

"Do you admire Mussolini?" the German asked, and his features were again relaxed and he looked young.

I hesitated, because I had never thought about it before. My father had been a Fascist; this I knew, as I knew he had died in Africa, for Italy, for Mussolini. In Messina I had seen the young boys in their black shirts and I had wanted to be among them; but that was a long time ago and I had

been very little. Now I was a beggar; a homeless
one; a child of the streets — of the Madonna; a little
fish, as the German in Naples had called me. I
shook my head, while I recalled the face of *Il Duce*
as I had seen it on the posters and in the news-
papers.

"Italian greatness, that died with Rome, too," the
German remarked.

"Greatness," I repeated the word the German
had said, and I realized that I pronounced it dif-
ferently.

"You are too young to understand." The German
smiled and looked out across the valley.

'What does he see?' I thought. 'Is it with sight
as it is with words, that each of us, looking at the
same view, sees something else?'

The German went back to his men and his gun,
and I walked to the edge of the stream, where
Mario was playing. The little boy was collecting
pebbles which he put next to each other in a pat-
tern. When he noticed me, he looked up and
smiled. I asked him what he was making. He
pointed to his work and said, "It is a church." I
nodded in agreement, though I could see nothing
but a row of stones; but it did not matter, for without waiting for my approval, Mario had returned to
his play, to his own thoughts, his own world. 'We
are all blind,' I thought, 'and we are all deaf, and
that is why we have wars.'

I walked upstream to our pool. I sat staring at

the water. Why had the coin meant so much to the German? And that emperor who had died long ago, why had his name been magic to him? I tried to remember the name of the emperor, Vespasian. Was there a St. Vespasian? . . . Still, it might be magic and protect one, as a St. Christopher medal would; then I reminded myself that it had not been made of gold or silver, and I laughed at the German for being so silly as to think that a copper coin could offer him protection. A wind came down the valley and the leaves in the trees rustled. The wind was cool, it would soon be autumn. But what did that matter to me, for we had a house. Why should I fear the winter?

17

DEAD LEAVES follow the wind and have no resting place during a storm. The twig that has fallen into the river goes where the stream carries it. The poor are like the leaves in the storm or the twig in the river: plaything of forces which they do not control, which they sometimes do not even understand.

We had heard that Salerno had fallen to the Allies, but Naples was still in the hands of the Germans. It was a morning like any other autumn morning. The sky was clear and the air had a little chill in it, a whisper of winter. Many a time American or English planes had flown over the valley. They usually flew so high that the Germans did not bother to fire at them; and the few times that they did, they hit nothing. That day four planes passed above us, much lower than usual and the Germans started firing.

We were all watching from the farm. "They are English," said the farmer. Little white clouds with black centers showed us where the German shells exploded in the air. To our astonishment one of the shells hit a plane and heavy black smoke streaked from one of its two engines. The other planes flew on, but the one that had been hit circled and started to descend.

Now we could see flames coming from the wing. The Germans fired again; but this time, I do not think that they hit it. As the plane passed above us, we saw a man jumping out of it; then with a great explosion the plane burst into small pieces that fell towards the ground.

"He is coming towards us!" the farmer called, as the wind carried the parachute and the pilot nearer and nearer to us in their descent.

I felt as one does at High Mass at Easter. You watch the priest and hear the singing. You are there and yet, in a strange way, you are not; the wonder of what you are seeing makes your arms and legs lame.

The parachutist was carried by the wind to the

valley, as the seeds of certain plants are carried in the summer. I think he saw what was going to happen to him, for suddenly he was waving wildly with his arms; then we heard the sound of the machine gun.

We were so shocked that we looked first towards the Germans. They had two machine guns: one on either side of their anti-aircraft cannon. Only one of them had fired. The young officer was standing there behind the cannon: he must have given the order.

When we looked back at the man in the parachute, he was no longer waving his arms, I think he was already dead. The Germans kept firing until the pilot disappeared into the gorge. Then they stopped and in the silence that followed, a dog barked at a farm nearby.

"Why did they shoot him?" I stammered.

The farmer wasn't listening. He ran across the fields, down through the vineyard, to the bottom of the gorge. I ran after him; but when I came to the edge of the field, I stopped for Mario was following me.

"Go back!" I shouted, but the boy continued until he was only a few steps from me. I turned and looked at him; his little face moved me in some way, and instead of scolding him as I had intended, I beckoned for him to come closer. He hugged me and I patted his head.

I saw the white cloth of the parachute down in

the valley. The farmer was coming up the hill slowly, the way a man does when he has finished a day's heavy work. When he saw me and the little one, he shook his head, to tell us what he had seen, before his words could reach us.

"He was dead." The farmer looked up towards the Germans. A group of them were descending the valley, going in the direction of the dead pilot. *"San Giuseppe . . . San Giuseppe!"* The peasant made the sign of the cross. Then he shook his head slowly from side to side, in wonder at what he had seen. "He was so young!" He caressed Mario's face, then he started back towards the farm, and Mario and I followed him.

At the house, the farmer's wife, their two daughters, and Anna were waiting for us. In response to their questions, the farmer only shook his head; then he disappeared into the kitchen. A few moments later he came out with a bottle of wine and a glass. He seated himself at the table, outside where we usually ate. He poured the glass full and drank it down without stopping.

"What a world." He had said the words to no one in particular.

"And didn't our son die like that?" his wife cried.

"How do I know!" the man shouted back at her. "Was I there? I've never been in Greece!" There were tears in his eyes, and I think that his thoughts were the same as his wife's.

"*Dio mio* . . . Why do they take our sons away?" she cried, as if only now she had heard the news of her son's death, though it was more than two years since she had received the telegram. The same kind of telegram that my mother had received. But maybe she hadn't believed it until now, until she had seen the bullets take the life of the English pilot.

"We shan't sell them anymore tomatoes . . . or any grapes," the youngest daughter screamed, her eyes flashed with anger. Being eighteen, she was only just a grownup.

Her father shrugged his shoulders. "We will sell them what they want," he said in a flat voice and filled his glass with wine. "They will lose that war; and soon, maybe they will be dead, too . . . Dead . . . Dead before they knew how to live."

Later in the afternoon, the miller came. He had not been at the mill for several days, for the grain harvest was long since over, and there was nothing for him to grind. "I have heard of it," he said, before any of us could speak. His eyes were shining with excitement; and I could not help noticing the difference between him and the farmer, whose eyes were sad with the knowledge of the day.

"We shall bury him, and give him the greatest funeral that has ever been in Sessa," the miller exclaimed.

The farmer's wife agreed and smiled; but the

peasant looked at the miller and asked, "Was that your idea?" The miller did not answer. "Was it yours, this beautiful idea?"

The miller appeared crestfallen, as people usually do, when they find that they are not the bringers of such good news, as they thought they were.

"These young men are scared. Bury the Englishman quietly; or you don't know what will happen. I tell you that they are scared! They could bring those guns of theirs to the funeral and make a lot more funerals necessary." The peasant was looking towards the Germans' anti-aircraft cannon. The soldiers had draped more branches on it since the morning, but one could still clearly make it out.

The Englishman was buried in Sessa Aurunca, and many people followed him to the grave, but a big funeral he did not get. The town was filled with refugees and a company of Germans had camped just outside. The refugees came from the south. As the Germans retreated north, they pushed them ahead of them: farther and farther away from their villages and farms. A few had come through the valley, families with bundles on their backs, poor ones. I thought of how a beach looked after a storm: filled with wreckage and garbage; war is such a storm and we are the wreckage.

We avoided the Germans. When we saw any of them, we would go into the fields, as if we had suddenly thought of some work which had to be done.

None of us went to the pool to bathe, for fear of meeting them. Yet I knew that sooner or later, there would be an encounter. It was easier to avoid the soldiers for they spoke so little Italian, one could pretend not to have understood, if one of them spoke; the officer was another matter. When we finally did face each other it was he who came to search us out.

He came one morning, just as we were getting up, the sleep was still in our eyes. I was on my way down to the stream to wash my face, when I saw him standing near the bridge, watching the mill. I started to hurry, but he called out my name. He looked tired as if he had not slept for many nights, and I noticed that he was unshaven.

"You have to go away from here," he said as I came near him. I looked puzzled, for I did not understand what he meant. "We are going to use the mill, and I don't want any little thieves around here." The officer had glanced away while he spoke, for he knew that we had never taken anything from them.

"Thieves . . . We are not thieves!" I said angrily; and I looked down at the ground, to keep myself from saying, 'Nor are we murderers, either.'

"Take your things away from the mill by noon."

"Have you asked the miller?" I said and our eyes met.

For a long time we stared at each other, finally

the officer bowed his head, "You don't understand war."

I did not speak, for what was there for me to say? Who understands war: the soldiers? the homeless ones? Mussolini? Or the leaders of the English and the Americans? No, nobody understands war, they only think they do. Maybe the earth that drinks up the blood understands it and says: "How foolish is man. Of all the animals that lives upon me, he is the cleverest and the most foolish."

"By noon," the officer repeated the command.

I nodded to signify that I understood, for the officer I did understand. He did not want the mill for himself, he just wanted us to leave it. He knew that when he gave the order to shoot the parachuting airman, he committed a crime, a sin; and we were the witnesses to it.

Anna and Mario came out of the mill. When Mario saw the officer, he smiled and looked relieved, for he had not understood why he must not talk with him and had only obeyed Anna and me because we had threatened him. Now he ran up to the German and asked for sugar.

The officer screamed at him, "Get away, little thief!"

The child was as confused as he was frightened, for he had thought the German was his friend. Angrily the man glanced at Anna and me; then he struck Mario on the cheek so hard that the child fell to the ground.

"Murderer! Murderer! Murderer!" Anna wildly screamed, and she ran to her little brother and picked him up.

"Get out of here!" the officer shouted and pointed with shaking hand towards Sessa and the land beyond it.

For a moment, I feared that he would kill us, shoot us as he had the pilot; but he turned on his heel and walked away.

We packed our few possessions and went to the farm, to tell what had happened to us. The peasant grew very angry and said that we could stay with him. It made me happy that he made such an offer, but I knew we couldn't accept it. He knew it, too. If we stayed we would bring trouble on him and his family; and when I refused, he did not argue with me. The Germans were like wasps who are starved. And as hungry wasps will attack and sting anyone — even each other — so would the Germans now think nothing of killing a whole family or destroying a village.

"They are mad," the farmer said and made the sign of the cross.

The peasant's wife cooked a good meal for us, and long after we were full, she kept ordering us to eat more. She gave us bread and cheese to take with us, and the farmer gave us ten *lire*, which he insisted was ours for the work we had done. I thanked him for it. It was very generous of him, for though he was free with food, he did not like to part with money.

The whole family stood waving to us, as we walked away.

I did not expect to see the German again, but when we came to the point where the path from the farm joins the road to Sessa, he was waiting for us. Quickly Mario took my hand and hid behind me. Anna looked the other way, pretending

not to see him. I felt frightened and looked at the
pistol in his belt.

"Here, it is yours." The voice of the officer was
stern.

I looked up at the little copper coin that he was holding out to me. "I gave it to you," I said.

"I don't want it! I don't want it!" As he repeated himself, the officer's voice broke and he sounded like an angry child.

I took the coin and stuck it in my shirt pocket. I was wearing one of the miller's shirts, which the farmer's wife had altered, so that it would fit me.

The German looked down at Mario, who was peeping out from behind me; and the child buried his face in my clothes and began to sob. For a moment, I thought that the German, too, was going to cry.

When he was gone Anna asked, "What did he give you?"

"A coin . . . A Roman one."

"Throw it away!" Anna exclaimed and turned around to look at the back of the German, who was walking towards the bridge.

"I shall keep it. It brought him no luck, for it was a Roman coin and he was no Roman." To myself, I said, 'But neither are you, Guido.' Then a moment later I answered my thoughts, 'More than he! I am more of a Roman than he.'

Suddenly I felt light-hearted. "Come, let's go."

"Where are we going?" Anna asked. Each of us had hold of one of Mario's hands.

"To Cassino!" I answered and this time I felt certain that we would get there.

18

FROM SESSA AURUNCA, we took the road towards Castleforte, and crossed the Garigliano River. There on its banks, among other refugees, we slept the first night. We froze. It was October and the nights were colder than usual for that time of the year. We were to be much colder that winter. Such is the wheel of misfortune that, although one cannot believe it will keep on turning, it does; and the suffering of yesterday becomes a memory of something hardly unpleasant compared to the misery of today.

"Is the little one sleeping?" Anna whispered. Mario was lying between us.

"Yes," I replied.

Anna lay on her back, her hands folded beneath

her head. She was looking up at the star-filled sky. "What if it rains, Guido?"

I knew that she was not thinking of tonight, but of the nights and days to come. "Maybe we can find a cave. There are lots of them in the mountains." Then I added, "Maybe we can stay in the monastery."

Anna smiled; this idea pleased her.

"I wish we could have stayed in our mill," I said sulkily.

Anna had closed her eyes. Mario had drawn his legs up to his chest; his face was turned towards me. I leaned over him and stroked his hair; then I, too, fell asleep.

"Give me that bread!" the man demanded.

I was sharing out bread to Anna and Mario. We had only half a loaf left. I shook my head.

"Give it to me!"

I was sitting on the ground, my left hand resting on the earth. Now I moved my hand over the soil until I found a stone. All the while I kept my gaze on the man's face. 'He has not eaten for a long time,' I thought. 'But if I give it to him, then we shall go hungry.' He didn't look like a beggar. "The little one . . . he needs the bread, too," I tried to explain.

The man grimaced and looked away. 'No, a beggar, he is not,' I thought.

"Give me . . . Give me a piece of it." The man's

tone which before had been angry and command-
ing, now became sorrowful and whimpering. I cut
off a slice and threw it to him. He stuffed half of
it in his mouth and then — I believe, it was because
he was ashamed of himself for not having obtained
all of our bread — he grunted and glared at me
angrily before he walked away.

I let the stone fall from my hand and looked at
Anna. I was worried that the man had frightened
her; but she was watching his departure unafraid.
Then I noticed that there was contempt in her
glance as she followed his movements down the
road. I felt sorry for him; for it must be a terrible
thing for a man to have to beg bread from children.

I stuffed the last pieces of bread in my shirt,
from now on we would have to hide our food.

"Let's go," I said and pulled Mario to his feet.
Anna smiled towards me, as she stood up, and instead of taking her brother's hand, as I had expected
her to, she took mine.

Soon we crossed the river; and the road to Castleforte branched to the left. We took the road to the
right and followed the river. Now we were in the
mountains. By evening the road left the river and
climbed to a village called Santa Andrea. I begged
from a peasant and he gave us a handful of chest-
nuts, but we had to eat them raw, for we could
not make a fire to roast them. That night, we again
slept outside.

There were other refugees on this road. Many

of them were people who had not carried poverty on their backs very long. To someone who did not know, we might all have looked alike: an army of dirty, ragged people. The German soldiers who passed us on the road could not see the differences among us. But Anna and I could. We knew by the way the women walked and the way the men glanced nervously at the mountains. But then, the Germans had changed, too; before they might have noticed. I saw in their faces not only contempt but hatred, as if they felt that somehow we were the cause of their defeat. Until Italy surrendered they had behaved as if they did not need our friendship, but they had always abided by our laws. Now groups of soldiers with trucks scoured the countryside. They took the farmers' livestock and even the little bit of seed that the peasants had hoarded for spring planting. They rarely paid for anything, and in several cases they had shot a farmer who tried to defend his cow or his horse. Sometimes we saw Germans with slaughtered animals on their backs, they never so much as glanced at us, but walked past as if we did not exist.

That afternoon we passed a group of German soldiers who were resting along the side of the road. They were eating and drinking wine. They were laughing; so I went up to them and held out my hand, to show that I was begging for food I pointed to one of the soldiers who was bringing a piece of bread to his mouth. Now their laughter stopped, and the soldier I was standing nearest to waved his arm towards the road, in this way telling me to go on. I acted as if I hadn't understood; then another soldier lifted his gun and aimed it at us.

'I wonder if he will shoot us,' I thought, but I was not really afraid, for how could anyone do anything so stupid?

Another soldier said something and the rifle was lowered. Anna, Mario, and I turned and walked on; but the soldier who had spoken called to us. Although I did not understand what he said, I stopped. The soldier ran up to us and presented me with a stone. The other soldiers laughed and the bearer of the gift beamed back. I judged him to be a fool, a clown who was used to entertaining his comrades. I would have liked to have thrown the stone at him, but I didn't. I put it down carefully at the side of the road and said, "*Danke schön* . . . Thank you." Without looking back I continued down the road. I knew only two phrases in German: please and thank you. The soldiers were no longer laughing.

A few minutes later, a voice called from behind, "You did well, boy. You did well!"

I turned and facing me was the strangest looking man I had ever seen. He was short and thin; yet his clothes must have been for a fat man. He held them together — both jacket and pants — with a piece of rope. On his head, he wore a hat with a feather stuck in it; and he had a beard. But for all of these, it was his shoes that held my attention. They had no shape at all and made his feet appear deformed.

The man laughed and held up one of his legs so that I could examine his shoes. "These are truly Italian shoes, made in the fashion of the day. In their earlier life, they were called a briefcase and as such carried books within. They protected Aristotle from the rain, which makes them almost holy. They are in truth the golden fleece, and my name is Jason."

The man looked so comical that we laughed. "Guido is my name and this is Anna. And the little one is called Mario."

The man, who called himself Jason, swept off his hat and bowed low before us. His head was nearly bald. "I am pleased to meet other travelers on this weary battlefield of life. Where do you hail from? What kingdom do you call your own?"

I grinned at the idea that I should have a kingdom. "We come from Naples."

"The Kingdom of the Two Sicilies," he said; then he frowned. "And I presume that Your Majesty is in strained circumstances like the rest of us."

I bobbed my head up and down; then I took a piece of bread from my pocket, broke a third of it off, and handed it to the man.

He bowed and reached into his jacket pocket for a small piece of cheese, which he divided into four pieces: one for each of us.

I bowed low and Anna entered into the game by curtsying.

"It is near noon," he said. "Let us rest and converse. Or as the vulgar say, 'talk awhile.'"

We entered a nearby field. The earth under the tree where we started to sit down was hard; and I would have looked for a better place but Signor Jason explained that the earth of Italy had grown hard from the war.

"Is your name really Jason?" I asked while I nibbled the cheese, trying to make it last as long as possible. "It is not an Italian name."

"What is a name? An opinion of your parents? A wish? How many little frightened and hungry Benitos does Italy have today? I might call my son Dante and yet he may never learn to read and write. A name should be a house for the soul, a flag on the battlements." He paused, then popped the rest of the cheese into his mouth. "My name is Luigi." He pronounced his name with disgust, which I could not understand, for I had known many boys in both Messina and Naples who had that name.

"I was a teacher. No, I am a teacher. The absence of a school does not take away my august title. I am a teacher, the most noble of professions, second only to the poet."

Anna started to laugh. Signor Luigi frowned, which stopped her from laughing but not from smiling.

"I think the young lady has never been to school, for surely if she had, she would have learned that the first rule of scholarship is not to laugh at your teacher . . . while he can see you."

"I have been to school!" Anna retorted angrily. "But you are not a teacher. You are just a person on the road like the rest of us."

Signor Luigi sighed and his face which before had been gay now looked sad. "It will soon be winter and the nights will be cold. What shall we do then?"

I shrugged my shoulders, for I felt confident that we could find a cave where we could keep a fire.

"We shall all die this winter," he said. "Oh, we shall all die."

The second time, he said the word, "die," I looked towards Mario, for I knew that the little one was frightened of that word as if it were a growling dog or a spider. "The Madonna will not let us die," I said and glanced at the teacher.

"Indeed not," he responded and he started to tell us a long story, which had neither head nor tail, but which made both Anna and Mario laugh. Later I was to recognize that this was the nature of Signor Luigi: he was either happy or in despair, optimistic or pessimistic; but never in between. It was noon or midnight. It was summer or winter. Morning and afternoon, autumn and spring, did not exist for him.

"And where are you traveling to? What is your destination?" We had been resting for more than an hour and our bread and cheese had long since been eaten.

"We are going to Cassino," I answered, while I hoped that he was going the same way, for I liked him and it would be well for us to have the protection of a grownup.

"The monastery . . . Yes, they would have to feed us there, for Christian charity's sake."

I agreed but I had already begun to doubt whether they could, for half the people we met on the road, said they were on their way to Cassino.

That night we rested near the Liri River, not far from the village called San Gergio. We had nothing to eat. It was to be a long time before we tasted real bread again. Anna and Mario fell asleep quickly, but I could not.

I sat down next to the schoolteacher, for he, too, was not sleepy. He told me about himself, how he had come from the north to teach school in the south, in Calabria. He mentioned that his family was wealthy and I wondered why he had chosen to live in the south, when the north is so much richer. While the schoolteacher talked of his life in Bologna, it occurred to me that he was a fool. For a moment I felt contempt for him, but then I remembered Father Pietro, the old one, and I thought that God was probably a fool, too. All over the world there were fools like him, and everybody laughed at them, but they were God's men.

I looked at Signor Luigi. He looked tired. How old was he?

"I think I shall sleep, Guido."

"Tomorrow, we shall be in Cassino," I responded and the teacher drew his jacket closer around him and sighed.

Beyond one of the mountains, I saw a strange light. I watched it; slowly the moon rose. 'They laugh at them, but they are also afraid of them and they hate them.' And the thought came to me, 'You, too, Guido, are a fool . . . You, too.'

19

"WHAT A WINTER!" Signor Luigi looked down at his feet and the snow on the ground.

"God must be angry with us," I said and looked out over the valley. We were standing outside the walls of the monastery, and below us stretched the snow covered city and plains of Cassino. It was the middle of January and the coldest winter that Italy had had for many years. The monastery was filled with refugees. There was hardly any food, yet each day, more people arrived.

Signor Luigi pointed to the valley beyond the town. We could make out the movement of troops. They were the Allied Armies, while in Cassino, itself, was a large force of Germans. "It would be best to leave," the schoolteacher said, "for soon there will be fighting here." But we both knew that we could not leave, for little Mario was sick. He was lying in a big room in the monastery which the monks had turned into a hospital. He looked so small beneath the blanket; only his eyes were large, large and bright as if the knowledge in them was unbearable. Mario was filled with fever.

"Maybe the Germans will surrender," I suggested.

"No." My companion shook his head. "That they won't do . . . Look at them!" Signor Luigi pointed to a German machine gun position a few hundred feet below us. "They are starving as we are. Lice filled as we are, and just as cold. They are suffering and all for nothing; but they won't give up. They no longer know why they are here, why they are fighting, but they will stay and be killed; for it is easier for them to die than to think." The last words the schoolteacher said with such venom that I turned to look at his face. At that moment one would have supposed that he never smiled; and yet it was only an hour since I had heard him joke with some children whom he was trying to make forget their hunger.

"We gave up. The Italian Army surrendered, why shouldn't the Germans?"

Signor Luigi laughed. "We Italians only wanted the victory march, the glory." The teacher hesitated; then he said very seriously, as if it were a confession, "I was a Fascist."

I shrugged my shoulders. "So was my father. So was everyone."

"Not everyone, Guido! One must never hide behind that . . . I had read history too closely, read of Caesar and the Roman Empire. I had not noticed that in the books there were white spaces between each line; the white spaces are there to remind you of the unspoken, the unwritten truth. When one only reads the words and does not read what is not written in the book, then one will never learn to understand."

Often Signor Luigi would speak in a manner that confused me; and then he would remind me of the count, who had given me ten *lire,* before he left Naples. "How can you read what isn't written?" I asked impatiently.

"When a child first has to learn how to read, the words seem to be a jungle of meaningless signs, all alike. Yet he learns to distinguish one letter from the other, one word from the next; and finally, he can read a whole sentence. It is more difficult and more painful to read what is not written, but it can be done . . . Remember, the speeches of Mussolini, I have heard him speak in Rome and I shouted with the crowd. I only thought of what he said, not of what he hadn't said. He spoke of Italian glory; he did not speak of death and starvation; he did not speak of cruelty; he did not speak of the blood of innocent people."

"Yes," I said eagerly, for I was beginning to un-

derstand what he meant; but the schoolteacher did
not notice, he was talking to himself.

"If I had known. If I had heard the unspoken
words. I would not have shouted with the rest of
the crowd. But I didn't hear them, Guido. Most of
us didn't and that is our shame." Signor Luigi shivered.

"It's cold," I said. "Let's go back." And I took his arm.

"The unspoken word blares like a trumpet now!" he whispered. "It blares like a trumpet."

I was looking down at Mario, who was lying on a mattress in the corner of the large hall.

"Is he going to die?" Anna whispered.

"I don't know," I answered.

She kneeled down beside him. Her lips were trembling. 'She is going to cry,' I thought.

I was wrong. She touched the forehead of the boy and looked up towards the ceiling of the room and started to mumble. She was praying. 'He will die,' I thought and I felt the tears come into my eyes, and then run down my cheeks.

"God wills."

I turned to see who was speaking. A monk was standing near me. I wanted to shout, no! for I could not believe that God had willed all that suffering on little Mario; but looking into the man's face, I saw that he was suffering, too; so I said nothing.

Anna had heard the monk, and she turned to him, her eyes dark with rage. "God wills it! God is a man. But Our Lady will not allow it, for she is a woman."

The monk smiled kindly; but his very kindness angered Anna the more. "It is God who rules the world and He will not listen to Our Lady; and that is why we have war. He has locked Our Lady in

Her room in heaven and that is why our prayers cannot reach Her."

The monk frowned unhappily. He felt so keenly the misery of others. I knew, too, that he gave away most of his scanty ration of bread.

When we were standing outside in the open courtyard of the monastery, Anna asked the question again, "Will he die?"

I intended to say no; but instead, I mumbled, "Yes."

"I knew all the time that he would die."

I looked at the girl with surprise; we had been together so long, and yet I did not know her. "How can you say that?" I asked angrily.

"A long time ago, I had an uncle; he died before the war. Our cat had kittens and my uncle drowned all but one of them. Well, that is the way God is; and Mario is one of the kittens who is going to be drowned." Her last sentence was jumbled together like a wail, and then Anna cried. She threw her arms around me and buried her head on my shoulder. I would have liked to have said something, for I felt she was wrong; but I, too, cried.

The monk who had spoken to us when we were at Mario's side in the morning came to find us that night in the corridor where we slept with tens of other people. The schoolteacher was telling us about history, of the times long ago. He was trying to divert us — and perhaps, himself as well — from the world around us. When Anna saw the monk, she asked, "Is he dead?"

The monk paused; then he said, "No, he is not dead yet; but I do not think that he will live through the night."

Anna rose. "I will sit beside him," she said.

"I will, too," I insisted.

Anna nodded; but when Signor Luigi asked whether he should join us, she shook her head. But when she had walked a few steps from him, she turned and smiled at the schoolteacher. "Thank you . . . Thank you . . ." she repeated.

Mario died shortly after midnight. He died in his sleep. Anna and I sat by him till the morning light came through the windows; then a monk, seeing that the boy was dead, made the sign of the cross over him, and covered his face with a blanket.

"He has gone home," the monk said to us.

'The earth did not provide much of a home for little Mario,' I thought; and for some inexplicable reason, I remembered him as he had been the first time I had talked with him, when he had been willing to eat dirt, in order to obtain a coin from the German officer.

"He is dead?" The schoolteacher looked at us and bowed his head; then he put his arms around both of us and pressed our bodies close to his, but he said no more.

20

IT WAS the end of January when the fighting
started in the city of Cassino. From the monastery,
we watched it. When I say we, I mean Signor
Luigi and myself, for Anna refused to walk outside
the walls of the monastery after Mario's death. She
worked in the kitchen with the monks; often we did
not see her from sunrise until we went to sleep at
night.

"How many people are still down there?" Signor
Luigi exclaimed, as we watched the puffs of smoke
from the far side of the valley. A battery of guns
had opened fire. The shells exploded near the railroad station. From where we stood, it all seemed
unreal, and I could not imagine what it must have
been like to be down there where the shells were
exploding.

"They are moving up the mountain," I observed,
pointing to a new German gun position that had

been built the night before, near the monastery.

"They have promised to stay outside the monastery. But for how long? And will the others know that they are not here? One day, Guido, those guns in the valley will be pointing up here. I know it. We should leave . . . We should leave." And the schoolteacher repeated the words I had heard him say every day since we arrived.

Today, for no particular reason his advice made me angry, "You can leave."

For a long time Signor Luigi was silent, then speaking very softly, almost in a whisper, he said, "Perhaps I will."

I looked at him with surprise for I did not really think he would go away without us.

"It is funny, isn't it, Guido, that I still want to live? I am a middle-aged man, ummarried, and am not even a very good schoolteacher, for I could not keep discipline and the children laughed at me; yet I want to live. I thought about it last night. I said to myself, 'Luigi, you should stay here and die.' But then I answered myself, 'No, I don't want to die.' You know what surprised me most, Guido?" The schoolteacher was looking out over the valley. "What surprised me most was that the voice was shouting at me. It was an angry voice. This morning when I woke up, I felt alive again. I wanted to teach school and knew that now I could."

"I don't know if Anna will leave, and I will

stay with Anna." I saw Anna's brooding face in my mind, and I shook my head.

"Go and talk to her, Guido. Soon there will be no food at all here. Ten people died this morning, among them an old man whom I spoke to only yesterday. I am afraid . . . I am afraid of the dead." The man who had called himself Jason, when we first met, looked down at his feet in embarrassment.

"I will talk to her; but if she won't go, then I shall stay, too."

"Go and find her. Talk to her now," Signor Luigi pleaded. A lone shell hit the side of the mountain, far below the monastery. "Soon the shells will be aimed up here; and the airplanes will come, too. Go and talk to her, Guido."

I went first to the kitchen to look for Anna, but she was not there. I found her in our corner of the long corridor; she was sitting with her back against the wall. Her legs were covered with the rags which we used for warmth at night. I sat down upon the floor beside her. She was rubbing one foot against the other. That is the worst part of chilblains: once your feet get warm, they start to itch and you rub them so hard that the skin comes off; then they bleed and you can't walk.

"If only we had some petroleum and a little olive oil," I said. But there was no petroleum and any olive oil would have been used in the cooking.

"There is nothing more, Guido. Nothing more

of anything. They keep a little for the children, but there is no more food."

While I was in the kitchen in search of Anna, I had seen the soup cooking. It was only water boiling with a little fat, a little oil, and a few laurel leaves.

"We must leave, Anna. Signor Luigi thinks that there will soon be fighting here."

Anna appeared not to have heard me. She looked down at her hands that were folded in her lap. "Do you remember, Guido?"

I glanced at her quizzically: what was it I should remember? But she did not raise her head.

"Do you remember the time Mario ate dirt?" Anna spoke very softly, "Do you remember?"

"Yes . . . Yes, I remember."

"Do you remember that I said he would die?"

"No," I answered uncertainly as I tried to recall everything that had happened that day in Naples, when I spoke to little Mario for the first time.

"I did say it, and I stole the coin from him."

Now because I did remember and could not contradict her, I said nothing.

"I am a bad person, Guido! A bad person." She looked up at me with eyes so sad, that I looked away.

"Anna," I whispered. "We are all bad. I once told you that I had no bread, when I had more than half a loaf hidden in my pockets."

My confession brought a tiny smile to Anna's lips; the first smile that I had seen on her face since Mario's death. I happened to glance across the corridor, to the place where an elderly couple, who had come up from Cassino a few days before, bearing two huge photographs, slept. The photographs, which were leaning up against the wall, were of a man and a woman, in their best clothes, staring out at the world with serious faces.

"The old man died," Anna whispered. "They found him a little while ago."

For the first time, I understood Signor Luigi's fears. "We must leave! If we stay here, this will be our grave, and I want to live. Like Signor Luigi, I want to live!" I took the girl's face between my hands, to force her to look into my eyes. "Anna, we are not bad. We are not good. We are the little fishes — too poor to be either. But we have a right to live!"

I pointed in the direction from which the sound of the guns came. "Are they not bad? Somebody told these people to kill each other, and to kill us. I didn't! Guido didn't!"

"You're good," Anna whispered.

"No! No! No! No!" For that was not what I meant, at all. "Will you come with us?" Anna tried to look away but I would not let her. "If you don't come then I will stay, too. Come for my sake."

Tears formed in Anna's eyes and then she whispered so low that I could hardly hear her, "I will go wherever you go, Guido."

Her words made me so happy that I jumped up and laughed. At that moment I felt certain that we both would live.

Before I ran from the hall to find Signor Luigi, I stopped in front of the photographs of the two old people. I wanted to break them, smash them: glass and frame; but what I did was to bow to them. 'No, Guido,' I thought, 'you are not good. You are a little fish, but your fins are strong; and you know the sight of a hook.'

Days had lost their names: Saturday, Wednesday, Tuesday, all were alike; cold and hungry. We left the monastery early one morning in the beginning of February. The mountains were covered with clouds. From down below in Cassino we could hear the boom of the heavy cannons and the firecracker sound of the machine guns.

We walked north and then east, trying to get through the lines to that part of Italy which we had heard had been liberated by the Allies. Every time we got near the front, we were sent back; twice by order of a soldier and many times by being fired upon. For five days we strayed in the mountains with almost nothing to eat. Then we found a wounded goat, which we killed and ate, while we camped for three days in an abandoned shepherd's hut. The goat had been so thin that there

was hardly any meat on his ribs, but the heart and
liver were good. If it had not been for the goat,
we would have died of hunger. Water there was
plenty of, for the earth was covered with snow.

It was a hard winter, a bitter winter. Anna had open sores on her toes and her heels from chilblains. We were dirty; our hair was matted with filth.

On the eastern slope of one of the mountains that surrounded the plain of Cassino, we managed to get through a German position. We were making our way down, on all fours, when a voice hailed us. "Stay where you are!"

He spoke in Italian, and we saw him almost at once. He was lying just a few feet below us, his body only half hidden by a bush. "There are mines," he warned. "Crawl this way. Don't stand up or they will fire on us."

I glanced back at the German position, all seemed quiet there; and then without quite realizing what I was doing I started to get up.

"Lie down!" he cried.

A moment later, we heard the shell above us, it exploded only fifty yards away, and the noise deafened us for a moment.

"Crawl after me," he ordered. "But crawl!"

We started down the mountainside. Two more shells exploded. They came from the valley. Neither of them came anywhere near us; and I realized that it was the Germans who were now being fired upon. We were between the lines; the place the soldiers call "no-man's-land" because they are still fighting over it.

"There," the man pointed ahead of us.

It was a cave. The entrance was narrow and partly hidden by a great rock, but it was high; and Anna and I could enter without stooping.

The cave, itself, must have been large, but it appeared small because there were so many people inside. We had come from the cold, from the fresh air of winter; therefore, the stench of the cave seemed doubly horrible. Everywhere people were lying. As in the monastery, most of them were women and children; and the only men were old.

More than a hundred people had sought refuge in this cave, when the fighting in this area began; now they had been here more than a month.

No one got up when we entered, but everyone's eyes were turned towards us. From a distant place in the cave, I heard a woman moaning.

"Has it come?" the man who had led us to the cave asked. Now that I could see his face, I realized that he was older than Signor Luigi.

One of the women shook her head. "Not yet."

"There is a woman who is expecting a child," he explained to us.

"You once talked of a cave, Guido," Anna whispered and took my hand in hers.

Mutely, I nodded. The cave I had thought about, had been like the one I had lived in, in Naples. The woman moaned again like an animal in pain. 'Some child wants to be born,' I thought to myself. 'Some child wants the world, even here, in this cold and dirty cave.'

The Rescue

21

THE FLOORS and the walls of the cave were cold and damp. Sometimes drops of water would fall from the roof onto the people sleeping below. The air was foul, but it was warm, as the air in a cow stable is. Food there was none of. The man we had met had been out looking for food, hoping to catch a stray goat or a sheep. When I say there was no food, it is true; yet the people ate. They stripped the bark of the small trees growing on the hillside; this they cooked or ate raw, if it was a very young branch; but that is goat food and will not satisfy a human stomach.

The night we came, the woman was delivered of her child; it was a boy. It is a strange cry that a newborn baby makes; it sounds like a cat.

"She has no milk," Anna said to me. We were sitting outside the cave, hidden by a rock from the valley below and by some bushes from the German gun positions above. It was here the cooking was done; but today we had not lighted the fire because yesterday the smoke had drawn artillery fire.

"If she gets no food, the baby will die," Anna remarked.

I said nothing, for I was thinking that in a few days many people in the cave would die. 'Babies,' I thought. 'They mean so much to women, even to girls like Anna.' Should one of the children in the cave die, there would not be the sorrow among the women that the death of this baby would cause. Yet the baby knew nothing. It was only three days old, just something that cried for food and warmth. When the baby had been born, even the oldest of the women, who otherwise never left their places, hobbled over to get a glimpse of the baby; and their eyes became young, and their lips smiled, and they nudged each other, mumbling, "*Madonna mia,* what a beautiful boy!" The old man did not join them. The men sat staring at the opening of the cave, for I think the cry of the infant made them feel more deeply their hopelessness. The cry of the baby told them that they had lost their homes.

"Someone has got to bring help. Someone has got to go through the lines and tell the soldiers in the valley that we are here." Signor Luigi had come out of the cave without our noticing him; his voice sounded determined.

I flung out my arm towards the stone. "Who are they, the soldiers below us."

"Does it matter? They are human beings," Anna said.

The days we had wandered in the mountains had taught me to fear all soldiers; everyone who carried a gun.

"They are the Allies, and they are no longer against us." Signor Luigi lowered his voice, "Besides, they are winning; they can afford to be generous."

"I will come with you!" I exclaimed; but the moment I spoke I realized that the schoolteacher had not yet said that he was going.

"The mines are the worst danger," he muttered; then he said more loudly, "Why should two of us die?"

The mentioning of the mines frightened me, for it seemed to me a terrible way to die. "There will be twice as much chance that someone will get through," I argued and looked at Anna. I expected her to try to stop me from going, but she sat silently staring at the ground.

Somewhere in the cave, a child was crying bitterly, a grownup voice tried to hush it. 'I am frightened,' I thought. 'But it is far better to try to get through than stay here. Soon they will start dying in the cave; and what then? We cannot even bury them!'

I heard a woman praying, calling upon Our Lady, and I smiled, remembering what Anna had said about God having locked Our Lady in her room in heaven, so that our prayers could not reach her.

"Mother Mine," I mumbled, "Go from Your room and help Your children, for if no one helps us, we shall die."

It was night, the schoolteacher and I were standing outside the cave, looking down into the valley, because of the snow, we could see in spite of the darkness.

"We must crawl down this mountain, keeping about fifty yards apart; so that if one of us is killed by a mine, the other one won't be hurt. And Guido, remember," Signor Luigi's voice was low. "Remember that if I am hurt, don't try to come and help me, just go on!"

We embraced and kissed each other on both cheeks; then the schoolteacher whispered, "I am still Jason, Guido; and below is the golden fleece."

I had crawled a few yards, when I heard Anna

behind me; before I turned, I looked at the disap-
pearing figure of Signor Luigi: he was moving
quickly in the snow. He had already started his
descent, I would have to crawl more to the left, if
we were to keep fifty yards apart.

"Guido," Anna whispered.

"I will get through," I said; and then hastily
I changed it, "We will get through, Anna. We will
get through."

Anna took my face between her hands and kissed
both my eyes. "Guido, you are my brother, my
father . . . You are all I have." Her voice was
shaking and I am sure that she was crying; but
she pushed me away and ran into the cave.

I could still see Signor Luigi. We were both
keeping close to the big stones and away from any
open places; not only from fear that we might be
seen by a patrol, but also because where the crust
of the mountain was covered with earth, it was
easier to bury mines in it. My hands were numb
from cold. Once when I saw the schoolteacher
resting, I rested, too, and ate some snow to quench
my thirst. My stomach pained me; but I don't
think it was from hunger, but from fright.

The lonely mountain was silent; and for a moment I was tempted to stand up and walk down it.
"Signor Luigi," I whispered, wishing that the
schoolteacher, whom I could no longer see, could

hear me. "Anna . . . Mama . . . Father Pietro
. . . sack of bones . . ." All the names of people
who had been kind to me, I whispered into the
night, as I crawled down the mountain.

The hollow, numb noise of a mine exploding
shook the earth and a flash of light blinded me.

"Signor Luigi!" I screamed. The schoolteacher
did not answer; but the German machine gun post
above opened fire. The bullets strayed far from
me. "Signor Luigi! Signor Luigi!" I whispered and
buried my face in my hands.

For a long time I lay motionless; but then the
coldness of the night made me crawl on.

A deep voice cried out in a language I did not
understand. I sought coverage behind a stone and
then I called out, "I am a child!" And then although there could be no other but an Italian child
on that mountainside, I called, "I am an Italian
child."

Again the voice said something, and I repeated
my words. Then from behind a pile of rocks the
soldier came out, his rifle pointed towards me. I
closed my eyes and crawled forward, while over
and over I said, "I am an Italian child . . . I am
an Italian child."

The hand of the soldier touched my face and
forced me to look into his. His face was as grimy
as mine. When he saw the fright in my eyes, he
smiled. It was not a happy smile and for that rea-

son it comforted me. The soldier held out his hand to me, and I brought it to my lips and kissed it.

The strange soldier pulled his hand away, as if I had bitten it; but then he was sorry and stroked my head.

For a long time, we crawled beside each other; then we came to a place where there were other soldiers. It was a machine gun position. The soldier who had found me spoke to an officer. The officer was very young. No one spoke Italian. The officer gave me a piece of chocolate. I ate it, and decided to beg some for Anna, thinking how surprised she would be when I brought her chocolate.

One of the soldiers motioned for me to follow him. Now we could walk upright. There were soldiers all about us; then I saw a truck, it had an American flag painted on the door. Finally we came to a house; it had been damaged and was hardly more than a ruin, but one of the downstairs rooms was still intact.

We had to enter through both a door and a curtain, which kept the bright light of the room from being seen outside. I think there were about ten people in the room. Most of them were standing, but there was one who was sitting at a desk and writing in a book. I was led up to the desk and then everyone turned to look at me.

The officer looked up from his book and asked me a question.

I shook my head, I had not understood him.

Then a young man whom I had not noticed before stepped up to me. "Where are you from?" he asked in Italian.

"From the mountain," I said and pointed behind me.

"Are there Germans there?"

"Yes," I replied eagerly, "there are Germans there."

The officer behind the desk now spoke to the young man; and I knew because his glance never left me while he spoke, that the officer was telling the Italian what he should ask me.

"Are you alone?"

"I came with another man . . . I came with Signor Luigi!" I cried. "Maybe he isn't dead; maybe he's just lying there on the mountainside. There was an explosion, but he had told me that I must . . . that I must go on."

The officer smiled kindly at me while I spoke; but when the young man had translated what I had said, he frowned unhappily. Then I told of the cave and all the people in it; and his eyes averted mine.

"They are starving! They are starving!" I repeated; then I turned to the young Italian and exclaimed, "Remember to say that they are starving. Tell him that there are more than a hundred people and there was a baby born there, four nights ago."

When the Italian had finished translating, the

American officer smiled at me, the same smile that had been on the soldier's face when he had found me in the mountains.

"Can you tell us where the Germans are?"

I nodded, for I sensed that the officer wanted to help us.

"We shall bring your friends out," the Italian said. He was a small, slight man, and he spoke Italian as people from the north do. "But not before tomorrow night. We must get rid of the German machine gun positions above the cave first."

'If only Anna knew,' I thought. 'If only she knew.' Again I thought of Signor Luigi and I begged the officer to send someone out to look for him; but this time, the Italian would not translate for me.

"He is dead, my boy. He is dead. And even if he were alive, we cannot ask these soldiers to risk their lives for him. But I tell you, I am sure, he is dead."

I started to cry, for I knew what he said was true. The American officer got up and came towards me. He rummaged in the pockets of his tunic until he found a piece of chocolate. But the Italian officer put his arms around me, drew me close to him, and I cried into the darkness of his uniform.

22

"THERE they come."

I was lying on the ground beside the Italian officer whom I had met two nights before. I strained my eyes looking towards the mountain where the cave was. "I can't see them," I whispered back. A pale light was coming from the east; it was beginning to be dawn.

"They will come soon," he said and smiled.

I smiled back. In some way this man reminded me of Signor Luigi; like the schoolteacher, he was unsure of himself. He had been kind to me. He had found clothes for me, and let me wash myself in the farmhouse which the officers used. The soldiers I had met were Americans; but at Cassino there were also Canadians, Englishmen, French, Poles, and other troops from countries far away I had never heard of before. The clothes I was wearing were soldier's clothes. They were too big for me, but they were clean; and for the first time in years my body was free of vermin.

"Can you see them now?"

The officer pointed and letting my gaze follow the direction of his finger, I saw black dots moving in the white snow, passing the darker rocks. They were not as far away as I had thought. I tried to pick out Anna among them, but they all looked alike.

"Why didn't they come earlier, it's getting too light," I said nervously; for surely if we could see them, so could the Germans.

"The patrol probably took long in finding the cave."

"Why wouldn't you let me go?" I demanded angrily. The officer only smiled and shrugged his shoulders. When I had said that I could lead the patrol to the cave, the American officer had almost been willing to let me go; but the Italian had frowned and said something to him in English. I had pointed out to them where the Germans were; and the whole day they had been firing mortar shells at their positions. Maybe, all the Germans were dead.

Now they were so near that I could distinguish the people from each other. In front were soldiers, behind them came Anna and most of the other children; then came the women and men. Finally, there were more soldiers and they were carrying those few of the old people who were too weak to walk.

A machine gun started firing from high up on the mountain. The people who had been walking in a crouched position, now straightened themselves and started to run.

"Anna!" I cried and jumped up.

Boom . . . Boom . . . Boom . . . We heard the hollow sound of mortar fire on either side of us, and the machine gun stopped.

"Guido!" Anna screamed.

I motioned for her to go on; but she ran to me and embraced me.

"Run!" an American soldier gestured angrily. Taking Anna's hand, we ran with the rest for shelter.

"Farther back, behind the lines, there is food," the Italian officer shouted, as he stopped in front of the ruined farmhouse.

"Signor Capitano . . ." One of the old men, who had been in the cave, called, "I am barefooted. Will they have some shoes?"

"Back . . . Farther back . . ." he motioned with his arms down the road.

But the people stood mutely looking at him; he spoke their language and the soldiers who had rescued them did not.

An elderly officer came out of the house. He was wearing a greatcoat; I had not seen him before. He looked at us and said a few words to the young soldier standing in the doorway. A few moments later, another soldier brought him a cup of coffee. He blew at it, to cool it; then he sipped it slowly.

"Good-bye," the Italian officer shook my hand. "And good luck, Guido."

"Thank you," I answered and was about to say, 'Good luck to you, too'; but the officer in the greatcoat called the Italian, and he turned to him at once.

The strange officer spoke loudly and in a very brusque manner.

"He said we were dirty!" Anna frowned angrily.

"How do you know what he's saying. He isn't speaking Italian."

"I know that word . . . Look, how he is looking at us! How can we be anything but dirty."

I smiled. We were already a distance past the farmhouse. I, too, had felt a momentary anger against the elderly officer, for although I could not understand what he said, the expression on his face had been most eloquent.

"Anna, one should not waste oneself with hate."

I could hear the sound of the explosions coming from the city of Cassino, which was miles behind us.

"Guido, why don't you hate?"

"I do hate, Anna . . . But not so much . . ." It was difficult to explain, for I did not want Anna to think I was good, that I forgave evil as Father Pietro had done. "The war," I started again. "The suffering, it must have a point and if I hate that man who only saw that we were dirty and did not ask himself why we were dirty . . . then . . . then . . ." Suddenly, I knew what I wanted to say. "Then I would be like him. And all we had gone through would be as meaningless as the seasons are to the sheep. It is understanding . . ." I said. "It is understanding that makes the difference between us and the animals. And when you understand you can feel a kind of happiness even in the worst misery."

"You mean that I should forgive the man for calling us dirty?"

I looked at Anna's matted hair and her face grimed with dirt. "Yes, you should forgive," I said; although that was not what I had meant. I had meant that one should understand. Suddenly, the figure of the old count, standing in his yellow dressing gown came to me. I laughed and thought, 'He would have understood what I mean.'

"Can I always stay with you, Guido?" Anna's voice trembled; and she glanced around at the refugees from the cave with whom we were walking. "I was so frightened when you left. I felt so alone. And then I heard the mine explode and I wanted to go and help you. But I was too afraid. The night was so dark."

I smiled. "We shall always stay together."

We walked in silence for a long time; then Anna, looking at the road ahead of us, said, "Where shall we go, Guido?"

I thought of all the roads we had walked. Was there none that would lead to a home, a place where we could stay? "There is an old count. I knew him in Naples. He gave me ten *lire* before he left the city to go to one of his estates. Maybe we shall find him; he was rich. I think he might help us."

"Ten *lire* is a lot of money. He must be very rich," Anna replied and nodded seriously.

"Yes, we shall try and find him," I said, for I knew that Anna always had to have a goal that would give our journey an end.

Epilogue

FOR MANY years after the war, its victims tramped the roads. I have seen them at night sleeping in doorways and among the ruins.

I like to think that Anna and Guido did well, that they became happy, that someone finally took the children in; not the count, but someone like the miller or a peasant who had land and no children of his own. Yet a kind wish is like a summer cloud, it brings no rain to the parched earth.